06

Comanche Captives

Comanche Captives

Fred Grove

THORNDIKE
CHIVERS

This Large Print edition is published by Thorndike Press®, Waterville, Maine USA and by BBC Audiobooks, Ltd, Bath, England.

Published in 2006 in the U.S. by arrangement with Golden West Literary Agency.

Published in 2006 in the U.K. by arrangement with Golden West Literary Agency.

U.S. Hardcover   0-7862-8801-9   (Western)
U.K. Hardcover 10: 1 4056 3862 1   (Chivers Large Print)
U.K. Hardcover 13: 978 1 405 63862 3
U.K. Softcover 10: 1 4056 3863 X   (Camden Large Print)
U.K. Softcover 13: 978 1 405 63863 0

Copyright © 1961 by Fred Grove
Copyright © renewed 1989 by Fred Grove

All rights reserved.

The text of this Large Print edition is unabridged.
Other aspects of the book may vary from the original edition.

Set in 16 pt. Plantin.

Printed in the United States on permanent paper.

British Library Cataloguing-in-Publication Data available

Library of Congress Cataloging-in-Publication Data

Grove, Fred.
     Comanche captives / by Fred Grove.
        p. cm. — (Thorndike Press large print Westerns)
     ISBN 0-7862-8801-9 (lg. print : hc : alk. paper)
        1. Comanche Indians — Wars — Fiction. 2. Large type books. I. Title. II. Thorndike Press large print Western series.
PS3557.R7C66 2006
  813'.54—dc22   2006010058

To Lucile and Bill

Chapter 1

At four o'clock the Austin stage, rushing and swaying, charged out of the cool streaky darkness, already dissolving to lighter shades across the rolling Texas country, and drew up with wheels smoking dust where the northbound from San Antonio, tongue down, awaited fresh teams outside Fort McKavett. There came the lifting murmur of sleepy voices, and two booted cattlemen and a young woman stepped down to stand dully in the swath of yellow light slanting through the doorway of the adobe station. Dust and mule sweat hung. At once an hostler hurried out to unhook the teams.

On these signals, hoofs sounded from the direction of the fort and the cavalry escort to Fort Concho swung up and halted, Sergeant Rooney and eight drowsy troopers. Not until then did William Forrest Baldwin limp forward.

"Morning, Rooney."

"Well! An' what brings the lieutenant back a week early?"

"Orders."

"Now that's a pity. Just when a man goes off to recover from a heathen's barb in his thigh." Rooney shook his head in sympathy.

"I'll be riding in a few days."

"In a pig's eye. How's San Antone?"

"Hot. But the beer's cool."

" 'Tis such talk of paradise that makes an old soldier want to go over the hill. By any chance did ye go out with a single girl?"

"No."

"Meantime, life goes on, Lieutenant. But I will not be meddlin'. Everything is still rosy up this way. Quahada captives gettin' fat on army grub. There's a war party out between here an' the post." Rooney did not sound excited, however.

"Well, let them come," Baldwin said in sudden bitterness, and he saw Rooney's stare fall across him.

The sergeant broke the pause deliberately, his tone confidential. "The rumors are thick again, sor."

"Fort Clark, I guess."

"They say that's next regimental headquarters. Whole outfit moves out right away to the border."

An established ease was between them as they talked on, watching the harnessing of six skittish mules for the north run. An uncommon amount of baggage seemed to be going into the rear boot and on the railed top of the Concord. Trunks, boxes, valises. Afterward, Baldwin climbed aboard and slammed the door and paused in the coach's gloom. The young woman and one of the ranchers occupied the rear seat, so Baldwin took the vacant place beside the other man. There was no delay. A fresh driver was mounting the box. He kicked off the brake, yowled at the mules and the coach lurched ahead for the San Saba crossing.

Sergeant Rooney's detail, trotting smartly, spread out on both sides.

Baldwin unbuttoned his blouse and leaned back, relaxing to the rocking motion on fore and aft leather thoroughbraces, smiling to himself over Rooney's outrage at the injustice of an interrupted leave.

Late breakfast at the next stage station was thick, greasy bacon, sourdough biscuits and coffee like quinine. Over the bent heads of the hungry men, wolfing their food beneath circling, sticky flies, Baldwin noticed the feminine passenger. She ate lightly, but without squeamishness. Now and then, when she glanced up, a pleasant expression entered her face, and it occurred to him that she was actually enjoying the company of these rough but gallant men. That the punishing ride from Austin, despite many discomforts, had been a new and stimulating experience, endured without complaint. Under the small flowered hat, her yellow hair lay knotted severely at the back, an austerity which extended to her high-necked traveling suit of sober gray serge. She was small and slender, almost slight, almost fragile, yet not. Her face, shadowed with fatigue, looked plain in the smoky room.

But in other ways she drew a man's attention a second time. Her large gray eyes were lively and serious, her features regular and expressive, her mouth full and placid. Her obvious air of breeding, so unusual on the frontier, caused him to speculate briefly. She might be twenty-two, he guessed, and probably bound for El Paso. Meeting his gaze, she returned a reserved nod of recognition, although it was the cattleman sharing her seat, erect, heavy, loud, shaggy-haired, who had assisted her from the stage.

Suddenly the meal was finished and the station-keeper spoke in warning to Sergeant Rooney. "Better keep a sharp lookout. There's a Dutch freight outfit up ahead somewhere."

Baldwin saw the attentive cattleman, the suggestion of a military carriage in his manner, make certain no one preempted his seat by escorting her to the stage. Now the four sat as before, the sluggishness of early morning upon them. And swiftly all coolness vanished from the scorched land and the sides of the coach seemed to confine and distill the suckling breath of the burning wind. A band of pronghorn antelope, their rump patches glittering white, appeared in the glass-bright distance, running free. Sergeant Rooney spread his fan of troopers wider, away from the rutted trail.

"How far is it to Fort Concho?" she asked.

Her question was unexpected and after a moment Baldwin realized that she had addressed him. Her voice was even and cultivated, carrying the soft accents of a Texas-born woman.

"Twenty to twenty-five miles."

She looked out on the passing landscape, a faint frown in her fine eyes. "It's true —

thee expects an Indian attack?"

"It's possible," Baldwin said, frankly surprised that she should doubt, and he felt a stab of exasperation, thinking that only an unrealistic Quaker would ask. Then, not wishing to alarm her, he modified his positiveness. "There is no cause for concern. We're armed and we have an escort."

The cattleman settled his wide frame protectingly, a sneer forming beneath the inverted oxbow of his black moustache. He fixed an uncompromising dislike on Baldwin's uniform. "Never saw blue-bellied Yank cavalry with much spine."

"I believe you have to catch Comanches before you can fight them," Baldwin said, distinct about it.

"Still takes *spine,* Lieutenant. *Spine.*"

Bald felt his temper fly. He curbed it, sensing more than the usual complaints of frontier civilians grumbling because overloaded troopers, limited to one grain-fed mount, couldn't run down Indians having a head start and stolen horses to switch to when pressed. Here something bitter and deep cut back into time. Baldwin made a guess.

"Did you happen to serve under General Hood?"

Large as he was, the Texan seemed to

12

grow larger. "I sure did," he replied, but the belligerent thrust of his jaw dropped a trifle in surprise. "Sergeant-major of infantry."

Baldwin nodded approval. "Hood was all tooth and toenails, wasn't he? I remember he came at us with everything he had around Atlanta. Never backed up. He was a fighter."

There fell a gap in their talk, broken by the rumbling rush of the coach and the cowman snoring on Baldwin's left, while the other Texan, thrown off guard, sat thoughtfully back, weighing the sincerity of Baldwin's tribute. "Wasn't expecting that from a Yankee," he said. "What you said is true — too true. Old Joe Johnston wasn't a bad general a-tall. Us boys hated to see Hood take over. We knew the killin' would get worse — and it sure did with Hood."

Further talk was difficult. The trail grew rougher, throwing the coach high on its fore springs and dropping it. Dust fumed up between the chattering floorboards. Holding a small handkerchief to her lips and nose, the Quaker girl swayed with the coach, as composed as she had been in the stage station. She would not complain. Baldwin had learned that much about her in this short time. Overhead, the driver

13

bawled and cursed his teams, his whip cracking. Presently, the stage leveled off and the wiry mules, finding smoother footing, went faster.

Some miles on, Baldwin felt a slowing down. Glancing out, he saw a freight outfit forted up, wagons circled tight, oxen inside. When the Concord halted and the troopers closed in, a sturdy blond man of middle age left the wagons. Excitement marked his gesturing arms and blurred his speech.

"Ach! Dey made a run at us early dis morning. I vas sleeping ven I hears shooding. I shoomps up! But pefore I can shood — dey savages are gone."

"Anybody hurt?" Rooney asked, looking toward the wagons.

"Nobody. But two oxes is dead," was the disconsolate and angry reply. "I dink ve stay here till dis blows offer."

Rooney smothered a grin. "Long time till snow flies, Dutchy."

"Tell him we'll send a detail out to escort him in," Baldwin called from the coach window. He recognized the outfit as contract freighters out of Fredericksburg, keepers of Fort Concho's lifeline, and as stubborn as the country was dangerous.

"No, py gott!" the Dutchman said. "Ve

14

camp here today — all day!"

"Then we'll send a detail out tomorrow. Let's go, Sergeant."

Rooney swung away, northwest, the coach lunged and the troopers spaced out again at regular intervals, a fresh alertness to their swiveled watching. On this spring day of 1873, the fooling live oak hills and deep, mesquite-dotted flats and draws suggested solitude and contentment to the naked eye, a remoteness from peril, a lulling fantasy if a man stared long enough to set himself a-dreaming of buffalo and bluestem grasses so tall they dragged the underside of a wagonbed. And yet Baldwin knew that out of those peaceful looking stretches unsuspecting trouble could boil up in the time it took to look off and back.

By now his snoring companion was jolted awake, quietly watching. General Hood's former sergeant-major hadn't spoken since leaving the stubborn Dutchman. He was looking left and right with careful eyes, intent on what might appear beyond the steadily trotting file of troopers. The young Quaker woman was silent, attentive, calm. They rode several miles up a climbing grade, gripped by the same watchfulness.

About two o'clock Baldwin looked east

and saw one rapid streak of dust rising from a draw. There was no need to voice a warning, for the cowmen had seen and were drawing heavy revolvers. Turning to her, he found Hood's Texan likewise turned.

She seemed to read their thinking immediately. "The panels of this coach are too thin to stop a bullet," she said. "I might as well sit up."

"Better get down on the floor," Baldwin said. It came out as a gruff command and he saw pink stain her cheeks.

"I prefer to watch. I believe, Lieutenant, thee said there was no cause for concern."

That had the big Texan grinning, enjoying Yankee unease.

Baldwin, feeling provocation for an instant, considered putting her down. But he turned to watch the east side again, and as he did so he had the incredible suspicion that she didn't believe him.

Out there the single spur of brown dust became a boiling whirlwind, racing nearer, angling to intercept the struggling stage. Baldwin could make out brilliant splashes of color that meant war ponies. Swift paints, claybanks, bays, whites, duns. Coppery shapes astride them. A bullet made frying sounds over the coach and he heard

16

the distant pop of gunfire. His patience broke. He swung around to hear the Texan saying, "Miss Pettijohn, you'll have to get down —"

Baldwin was not so gentle. He barked, "You can't stay there!" and he reached for her. Before he could touch her, something in her eyes checked him.

Her face was flushed, either from excitement or anger or both. He couldn't tell which. Wordlessly, she slipped to the floor.

At the window Baldwin saw the nearest trooper fall back, leaving the passengers an open field of fire. Rooney had spaced his men well, forming them in a half-moon shield protecting the plunging stage on the attack side. As the range shortened, carbines started banging. The driver's steady yowl, urging, damning, pleading, changed suddenly, higher, lifted to the terrible Rebel yell Baldwin remembered, "Yip-aw — awww!" The frightened mules, as if sensing a greater danger behind them, fled with a quickening perverseness.

When it seemed at the final moment that the charging mass would drive headlong into the troopers, the foremost bunch of Indians swerved aside with the precision of a regimental drill team. Another followed. Another, riding demon-like, screeching,

17

squalling. And briefly, through the roiling dust, Baldwin glimpsed tossing head-dresses, horns, red flannel and ocher-streaked faces before the riders, swinging to the far sides of their painted mounts, began a drumming run past escort and stage, firing under pony necks.

Powder smoke bit Baldwin's throat. He pressed off his shots at a meager arm or leg or face and heard bullets striking back on the hickory framework of the weaving coach. He saw Private Fenwick slump forward, but hang on, maintaining the skirmish line.

Howling like mad wolves, the Comanches swept by, circling, and in moments they raced in again on the slower coach, the fleetness of their ponies unbelievable. One acrobatic brave on a claybank, red hands emblazoned on both its churning shoulders, avoided the screening carbine fire, cut inside the flankers and rode straight for the coach, rifle upraised. Troopers couldn't fire, then, for fear of hitting the passengers.

A hideous screeching filled the coach.

Baldwin and the burly Texan fired almost together and the yellow-streaked face fell away.

Now the Comanches began swarming

like angry bees, making tight circles on the flanks to lure green troopers into chasing them. One could stand temptation no longer. As the Indians in front of him pulled away, he yelled and charged them.

Sergeant Rooney, appearing to expect such rash action, was jumping his mount forward even as Baldwin, unheard, shouted the trooper back.

For some rods Rooney didn't gain. He bogged the spurs. His tired horse leaped out and then, cutting across, Rooney reached the rump of the trooper's animal. Rooney urged his mount up again. For a straining moment both horses were running side by side. Reaching out, Rooney hauled hard on the reins and the horses pulled up in a snarl of dust, head-fighting curb bits. Rooney gestured emphatically toward the Indians, who were slowing down and looking back. They made taunting signs. Rooney shook his head. His jaws were working as the two returned.

Baldwin, watching the scene, thought he could almost recite the sum and substance of Rooney's lecture on survival: "What're ye aimin' to do, boy? Commit suicide? Follow them heathens into the brush so they can lift yer hair? They want ye to kite after 'em!" In a calmer, persuasive tone:

"Now, lad, ye've got too much savvy to play their bloody game. Let's rejoin the detail."

The strung-out troopers closed up, going much slower, in tighter files flanking the coach. One more feinting rush developed. One more yammering chorus of insulting yells for the pony soldiers. And suddenly the Comanches were melting into the distance, and the mocking reaches of undulating land appeared as harmless and empty as before.

Baldwin looked about. She was sitting up, her face pale but controlled through the dust smudges. She did not return his glance. Stage and escort stopped and Baldwin got out, giving a hand as they took Private Fenwick down from his bloody saddle, opened his blouse and tipped him a swallow from his canteen. Fenwick had taken a bullet above the belt. His face looked pasty under his browned coloring.

Rooney rose with a savage mutter, turned his back and crossed himself. Fenwick was hardly more than a boy, just six months off a Missouri farm.

"Put him on the stage," Baldwin said, admitting his own helplessness in the order. "See what we can do there."

A woman's voice said, "Please wait. Let me see."

She kneeled down and felt Fenwick's pulse in a practiced way. She studied his blanched face, touched it. She stood up, her manner grave and hurried as she said, "Make shade — don't move him yet," and walked rapidly to the off side of the coach beyond the troopers. Baldwin heard quick ripping sounds, after which she returned with strips of white, ruffled cloth. "These petticoat bandages will have to do," she said, stepping past him.

After Fenwick was carried to the coach, Baldwin took the wounded man's horse and mounted stiffly, a difficulty that galled him. He drove the detachment hard.

Before sundown he led out across a broad prairie littered with dog towns and saw landmark twin mountains rearing flatly above the plain west of the fort and the grimy little settlement of Saint Angela at the junction of the three Conchos. He wondered how his fair passenger would react to its miserable dugouts, picket *jacals* and the lone hotel, a brazen pretender to accommodations for weary travelers surviving the waylaid trails to the south.

Rolling through a thick stand of massive pecan trees bordering the South Concho, the stage made the crossing and pulled into the environs of the stone fort.

A surgeon was summoned.

After Fenwick was removed on a stretcher, Baldwin rode to the Quaker passenger's side of the stage. "Thank you," he said briefly and included an apology he didn't feel she deserved in view of the circumstances. "Sorry I had to be abrupt back there. I thought the situation warranted it."

"Oh, thee needn't be," she said, showing him a cool cheerfulness. "Besides, thee's a firm man, Lieutenant."

The Texan was watching, slow-grinning again.

Baldwin nodded stiffly to her, touched his hat and rode to headquarters.

Colonel Ranald S. Mackenzie, 4th Cavalry, commanding, could be irascible when old wounds troubled him, which was often. Baldwin found him unchanged not long before Retreat, fretful and impatient while listening to details of the attack, the wounding of Private Fenwick and the Dutch freight outfit's dilemma.

"Sergeant Rooney handled the escort extremely well," Baldwin concluded. "In addition to stopping one trooper who started to chase after the Indians."

"You would like to see Rooney promoted, wouldn't you?" Mackenzie said, with a quick look of understanding. "I might add that I share the same desire. The problem, Mr. Baldwin, as you well know of course, being an old hand, is that every officer in the regiment has taken a drastic reduction from his war-time rank, yourself included. I have former brevet captains and colonels serving as second lieutenants. I have two former majors serving in the ranks because they can't let whisky alone." He scowled unhappily. "Rooney, bless his Irish heart, in all probability will finish out his enlistment as a sergeant."

The colonel paused and an expression bordering on distaste gathered in the lean, stern face, clean shaven except for sideburns curving low on the aggressive jaws. "You're wondering why your sick leave was cancelled, and I am prepared to answer that now. First off, it's not involved with moving regimental headquarters to Fort Clark, as you probably thought." He delayed again, pressing his thin lips together. "At ease, Lieutenant. Get off that game leg."

Baldwin flushed and sat down, wondering if Mackenzie ever missed one single detail about a man. At the same time, it wasn't like the colonel to hesitate in any degree, whether giving orders or fighting Indians.

Mackenzie's mouth firmed. "Mr. Baldwin, you will not accompany the regiment at this time for several reasons. Number One: you're not fit for active duty —"

"I rode Private Fenwick's mount in."

"I'm aware of that. But you didn't mask your limp effectively enough. I saw you dismount and I saw you hobble the short distance across the parade to headquarters. When you came in here, however, you managed to appear remarkably improved." He lectured on, cutting short Baldwin's protest. "You were afraid you'd miss the border campaign and you were right. Number Two: you are being assigned to accompany and direct the removal of the Quahada Comanche captives to Fort Sill in Indian Territory."

For a shocked moment Baldwin stiffened as from a stunning blow. He stared sickly, in stupefied silence. When he did open his mouth to speak, Mackenzie lifted a denying hand.

"Don't interrupt, Mr. Baldwin. It's a nasty job. I know that and I know what you're going to say. Unfortunately, there is no way I can change the order. It's from General Sheridan himself and you are my personal choice to carry it out."

At last, Baldwin could speak. "I don't understand, Colonel. You say I'm not fit for active service. Yet I'm to wet-nurse these wild Quahadas. How, in Heaven's name?"

"You can ride in an ambulance until you're able to mount. Reason Number Three: you know Indians, Baldwin. You don't like them, true, but you understand them. Actually, your rather intense feeling about them" — sympathy stood in Mackenzie's eyes — "is an advantage, I think. For a Hoosier State man you've shown unusual savvy with Indians. You've handled Tonkawa scouts. These Comanches know you as well as you do them. They know you mean what you say: you helped capture them on McClellan Creek and you were in charge of bringing them to Fort Concho."

Baldwin eyed him warily. The colonel had a way of making the most unpleasant duty sound inviting. So he was doing now, painting attractive pictures and lining up his arguments like a battery of field pieces. Baldwin said, "I think I know how to fight

Comanches a little, Colonel. Coddle them — no. I refuse to do that."

"Did I say *coddle?*" Mackenzie's voice was clipped. "You know me better than that. So, Mr. Baldwin, you will proceed accordingly, keeping the captives under the strictest surveillance at all times. Particularly that old devil, Hard Shirt. It is most important that they all reach Fort Sill in good condition. It seems Hard Shirt has become an important personage. The Society of Friends has convinced Washington that his safe arrival — because he's some sort of sub chief — along with the women and children and the few other bucks — is vital to keeping the main body of Comanches peaceful this summer and demonstrating the government's good intentions. Part of the so-called Peace Policy."

Baldwin's bitterness leaped out. "I wonder if the buck who shot Private Fenwick today ever heard of the Peace Policy?"

"At any rate," the colonel said wearily, "General Sheridan has instructed me to give full support to the plan. The captives should be fairly co-operative, since you will be returning them to their relatives."

"Unless they try to sneak off to the Staked Plains. That's their home. Not the Fort Sill reservation." Baldwin was staring at the floor. Already he could see the shape of many things.

"You must prevent that. . . . Now, you will have the first platoon from you own Company C as escort —"

"Why, Colonel, it must be four hundred miles or more to Fort Sill," Baldwin said, rising. "We'll be traveling through settlements where they shoot an Indian on sight. Any war parties we meet won't know we're taking these people back to release them. No more than today's Comanches."

Mackenzie nodded gravely. "I've taken all that into consideration. I have."

"You recall, Colonel, it was a different situation when we brought the captives down last year. The whole command was along. Now just one platoon —"

"Nevertheless, because of the regiment's commitments along the border I can spare you only one platoon, Lieutenant."

"In that case, sir, I request Sergeant Rooney from C's second platoon. He knows sign talk and he can grunt pretty fair Comanche."

"Captain McGregor will protest."

"Let him! Or give me a full company." Baldwin tensed, waiting. He was fighting for a man he needed desperately and he sensed that the colonel knew it.

Mackenzie considered at length before answering, tugging on the skin of his bare chin. "I see you've learned to swap and barter, Mr. Baldwin. In turn, I prefer not to make it any more difficult for you. Very well. You may have Sergeant Rooney. I'll notify McGregor and pretend I've lost my hearing. Meantime, you get with the quartermaster. Estimate rations, forage and wagons. Better hire Mexicans to do the cooking for the Indians. Be less wasteful."

Despite his unwillingness, Baldwin discovered that the colonel's contagious enthusiasm was affecting him a little. Confound Mackenzie! He could always impart that to a man, regardless.

"There is yet another detail, Lieutenant." Mackenzie's austere face had resumed the hesitancy again. "A teacher is going with you."

Baldwin blinked. "A teacher?"

"To be more explicit, a teacher-missionary for the Indians around Fort Sill. A graduate of Swarthmore College, no less."

Baldwin's thinking was split between this unforeseen turn and the countless details ahead of him. He said offhandedly, "I'll look out for him. One more man will help that much, if he doesn't fool with the Indians."

Mackenzie had a strained look. "It isn't a he, Lieutenant. It's a woman," he said, his expression that of one forced to release a bombshell.

"My God, Colonel!" Baldwin said, a tide of complications swamping his mind. "What next?"

"That's all, which is enough, I believe."

"Where is she?"

"She was due on the afternoon stage from Austin. A young Quaker woman by the name of Miss Rachel Pettijohn."

Chapter 2

Up close, Baldwin thought, they looked unkempt and listless, all except the small
bronzed boys, naked as tadpoles and active
as half-grown antelopes, and the little girls,
long-haired, in breechclouts, their older sisters in buckskin dresses. There seemed no
thought of clothing the coppery colts until
they reached the age of eight or nine, when
on came breechclouts, leggings and moccasins. The women and bucks straggling back
and forth from the wagons presented faces
of stolid indifference. But Baldwin knew
the defiance was still there, as strong as ever
despite a fattening winter quartered in Fort
Concho's corrals. Defiance and distrust.
For these were the Wild Ones. Quahadas.
They detested every white man's tracks and
with that memorizing hatred, he was aware,
went his part in their humiliation and defeat at McClellan Creek.

Sergeant Rooney rode up. "I counted a

hundred an' three, sor."

"How many bucks?"

"Seven. Five old heathens, two middle-aged ones."

"Did you tell them where they are going?"

"First thing, Lieutenant. They don't mind that. But they don't like the wagons. They want ponies an' drags to haul their stuff on."

Rooney was a blue-eyed, not easily excitable man in his early forties whose saddle-colored face was generally set in stern lines from his years as a noncom, testified to by four hash marks on his sleeve. He looked short and squat, almost undersized, a miscalculation sometimes discovered too late when angry eyes, on closer inspection, noted the battle-scarred fists and that most of him was gathered in the keg chest and in arms as muscular as a company farrier's. Now he cocked his head and scrubbed the stiff matting of his cropped moustache, his severity relaxing in a wry grin. "Old Hard Shirt, particular. Raisin' hell this morning, he is, Lieutenant. Claims it's a comedown for a mighty warrior and a famous hawrse thief like him to have to ride with a bunch of women. Says it will hurt his prestige as chief with the Great White Father in Washington."

"It's a shame about that old murderer," Baldwin said, all sarcasm. "Give him a pony and you know what would happen. We'd be missing an Indian. Personally, I don't believe Hard Shirt's a chief at all. Through his numerous relatives at Fort Sill he has just succeeded in making the Quakers, and the Indian Ring, think so. Regardless of what I think, however, he is our most important prisoner. As wagon-master, you will be moving up and down the column a lot. Observe him closely. Break up any fraternizing. These Indians are actually prisoners of war, not passengers in a wagon train."

Angry voices drew Baldwin's attention to the line of wagons near the corrals, where he saw troopers trying to coax a family of Quahadas inside a wagon.

Rooney made a groaning sound. "It's Hard Shirt again."

Lieutenant and sergeant went forward together, briskly. Baldwin's frayed patience was raveling out fast. He and Rooney had been attempting to organize the column since five o'clock. It was now seven and the Texas sun was beginning to scald. Time, Baldwin realized once again, in frustration, held little importance when a Comanche's belly was full of army rations. *Why load everything at once like the humorous white man? Why carry heavy loads when one object at a time is easier?*

Old Hard Shirt stood like a column of weathered brown sandstone, arms folded, naked except for breechclout and bead-embroidered moccasins. His coarse, greasy, graying hair was braided into a single scalp lock adorned by an eagle feather. Although not large and of indeterminate age, he looked muscular and active. His broad, wrinkled face was proud, his thin lips arrogant. Pock marks increased his fierce bearing. Black, glittering eyes spewed scorn from under plucked eyebrows. He stood absolutely still and aloof, by no slightest sign indicating that he recognized the existence of despicable white men around him.

Baldwin made the sign for Talk.

Hard Shirt ignored him.

"Rooney," Baldwin said, "your Comanche is far better than mine. Tell him he's holding up the train."

Rooney's right hand described fluid signs. Hard Shirt replied tersely, like a knife cutting. Baldwin understood: *pony — ride pony*. Further, that the Comanche spoke to Rooney alone. Hard Shirt had picked up an uncertain knowledge of stable English from troopers during the winter. But to demonstrate his disdain, Baldwin saw, he was refusing to talk in the white man's tongue. Now, Hard Shirt jabbered Comanche.

"He says," Rooney began, striving to be matter of fact, "he's one heap smart Indian an' savvies our lingo easy. As chief, however, his talk today will have to be the Indian way."

"You mean he won't talk to me directly. I got that. He said something else about the pony. What was it?"

"He . . . wants to ride with the leaders, as he calls 'em, at head of the column."

"Remind him he was afoot when we captured him. We have not extra horses for captives."

Rooney was so long relaying Hard Shirt's reply that Baldwin asked, "Well — what did he say?"

"He says," Rooney said, looking uncomfortable, "he is a great chief. By rights he ought to have the lieutenant's hawrse and uniform an' the lieutenant ride in the wagon."

"Tell him I know he is a mighty chief. But I am a bigger chief. Therefore, he will ride in the wagon with the squaws."

Hard Shirt gestured in circles, all

34

around, and slapped his chest.

"Sor," Rooney reported lamely, "he says he's bigger because he has more people here than the lieutenant has pony soldiers."

Baldwin stiffened. Such ridiculous chest-beating could continue endlessly. He dallied no longer. "You troopers there — put that Indian in the wagon!" No one moved and Baldwin bellowed, "Pick him up and put him in!"

Two husky troopers, awkward and reluctant, moved to each side of Hard Shirt and hoisted. The Comanche stayed board stiff, arms still folded. When a trooper glanced back in silent appeal, Baldwin spoke as if directing the loading of a forage wagon. "Go ahead. Take him over there and let down the tailgate. Load him on like a sack of corn. If he prefers to ride in that horizontal fashion, fine. After the bumping starts, I have an idea he will change his mind."

Baldwin reined away, a multitude of details snarled in his mind. "I figure we'll be doing well to average fourteen miles a day at first. We will dispense with trumpet calls, travel as quietly as possible. Don't detail any Mexican drivers on the commissary wagons. They might forget to look if a

Comanche sticks his hand in the sugar. We've a few civilian teamsters to fill out with. I want most of the platoon mounted up at all times. As for rations, the quartermaster informs me there is nothing we can depend on between here and Fort Griffin. So I've estimated everything on that basis. Forage, too."

"About mess, Lieutenant. Same as last time? Have each wagon bunch do its own cookin?"

"Worked best, didn't it? We'll do that. The Mexicans understand they are to handle the cooking for the Indians. Distribution of rations will be on a daily basis. You remember what happened coming down from McClellan Creek?"

"They wolfed a week's rations at one settin'."

"It will be four pounds daily issue to the person. Adults and children."

Rooney bent him a curious look. "Ye're generous, Lieutenant."

"No. I just prefer to keep them fat and happy. I'm not overlooking the chance of buffalo. A little hunting at the proper time. No doubt we'll be traveling light by the time we reach Fort Griffin."

He looked up and paused. Three troopers idled beside a wagon in front of the forage sheds, taking no part in loading sacks of shelled corn.

"Van Horn, Stecker and Ives," Rooney said, his dearth of enthusiasm telling an old story. "Just out of the guard-house. Van Horn for bein' drunk again. Stecker for fightin' in ranks an' insultin' language to Cawpril Higgins. Ives for gamblin'."

"I would leave them behind if we weren't undermanned."

"I'll get 'em started again."

"On the contrary," Baldwin said, frowning, "maybe I should. Ives has been grouching hard since I broke him. You hurry up the Indians, Sergeant."

Nearing the wagon, Baldwin saw the three leave and saunter slowly into the sheds. He had expected that and when Stecker and Ives appeared, lugging one sack between them, he was waiting. Van Horn trailed after them, pretending to help another trooper.

"Stecker," Baldwin said, after the pair had deposited the sack, "you and Ives single off. One man to a sack. Everybody. We're way behind."

Stecker's eyes fell on Ives, a slanting, I-told-you-so look, and he turned to go back.

Baldwin said, "Did you hear the order, Stecker?"

"Aye, I heard you, Lieutenant," said the trooper, halting and pivoting around. Stecker was a strapping man, boastful, profane, his reputation brawler and bully. His long, straw-colored hair showed under his felt campaign hat, his high cheekbones bore pitted scars and his large nose, flattened crookedly, lent him an additional pugnacious look. It wasn't how he had replied, Baldwin decided, it was what he had left unspoken. For there was a dangerous mixture of the unpredictable and the surly and the threatening about Stecker; his rebellion lay like a pointed rock just below the surface of his sullen manner, more sensed than seen, yet invariably there. Baldwin felt this again as the man presented the edge of his heavy-lidded, quarrelsome eyes, then moved on.

Ives, seldom lost for comment, complained, "Lieutenant, we don't like sweatin' for a pack of filthy Indians."

"If it wasn't Indians, it would be something else to grumble about," Baldwin said. Having seen enlisted men come and go, he thought he understood Ives better than Ives did himself. The frontier brought out a man's strong and weak points and Ives didn't measure up. He was more intelligent than Stecker, and older, but he had become a grumbling sower of discontent. He was fat-bodied in a regiment of mostly lean men, as round at the waist as he was at the chest, and his quick hands looked as soft as a milk maid's. But the eyes told the man: feline, resourceful.

"No matter what you have neglected today," Baldwin said, "it won't get you back in the guardhouse where you can dodge going on escort duty. Now move along."

"Guardhouse was the last place I had in mind, sir," replied Ives. His cat's grin came as he went off.

Private Van Horn paused, en route to the sheds. "The weight of command rests no easier, does it, Lieutenant?" he said in a speech brushing mockery.

Baldwin regarded an angular face, once near-handsome, now a ruin of blotched veins. Van Horn's critical, bloodshot stare had dirt in the eye corners. His sandy moustache showed yellowish stains. He stood slouched, weaving slightly. His soiled blouse was unbuttoned.

Baldwin felt a twinge of sympathy. Still, he couldn't swallow the superior air, the open, nourishing resentment and accusation he saw in this educated man, who, like himself and only a few years older, had reached brevet major late in the War and, also like Baldwin, had been a first lieutenant until one year ago.

"Not," Baldwin replied, "when former officers contribute to neglect of duty."

"A man takes a drink now and then and is reduced to ranks." Van Horn's mottled hands jerked. "Is that justice? By God, you know it's not!"

"I had nothing to do with your demotion, Van," Baldwin said and regretted his own lack of restraint for providing Van Horn the chance to expound. "The day you take yourself in hand, I'll be glad to recommend promotion to sergeant."

"Sergeant!" Van Horn exploded through a sorely wounded pride. "By God, sir, I shall be raised to my deserved rank — the rank you hold — or not at all."

"Come on, Van. You've no one to blame but yourself. You know that."

A hidden look stabbed the inflamed eyes. "You — you're to blame! I should have known! You told Mackenzie! Well, sir, you had best be on your guard." He drew himself up and marched past, for the first time striking a military pose.

Baldwin was too astonished to retort, stunned by the naked arraignment of himself that he saw. Watching after Van Horn, he knew he could never rely heavily on the man. On the three of them. They were misfits — Van Horn bearing like a public cross the claimed injustice of his demotion, spluttering exaggerated, self-asserted conceptions of his importance as a field officer, while denying his unreliability and refusing to accept restrictions on his moody drinking. Behind Stecker, so barrack rumors ran, was a term in prison for mutiny in the navy, and Ives appeared to be marking time until something more attractive than army food, clothing, shelter and pay-day gambling proceeds presented itself.

A bitter knowledge rubbed. Untrustworthy as these men were, Baldwin required their grudging services; which, in admission, was a kind of sorry commentary on the army's cream and dregs and the anonymous identities of the faceless men who helped fill its roster rolls.

Likewise, in their unmasked eyes, Baldwin had seen himself as though in a mirror. He was on the other side. He was an enemy, tolerated only until he forced them beyond the short limits of their questionable loyalty.

He rode back, in heavy thought. The ache in his thigh started again. He could see Rooney here and there, ordering, dismounting to assist with a team of fractious mules, now pointing out a wagon for more languid Indians to enter. Rooney crossed over.

"Formin' up pretty good, Lieutenant. Got all the heathens' wagons in the center, like ye ordered. Where we can watch 'em."

"Does Corporal Higgins understand about the rear guard? Watching out for stragglers? Some Indians will try walking once they tire of the bumping. I don't want any stops for sore-footed Comanches falling behind. He is to keep our rear closed up, always. Same as a file-closer."

"We went over that. He knows what to do."

Impatient to be off, Baldwin sent a checking glance up and down the column. His own Dougherty ambulance, which he intended to board and rest his leg in after the train was under way, sat ready at the head of the line. Around the second Dougherty, its mules hitched, its carefully selected trooper driver waiting, there was a singular absence of activity.

Baldwin's temper tore out. "Now where the hell is Miss Pettijohn?"

"Comin' down the road right now, she is."

Indeed, Miss Pettijohn was arriving. Baldwin scowled at her beside the Mexican buckboard driver, and something in his looking must have reached across to her, because he saw her look back. He scowled again, at her baggage, at the many sizes and shapes of boxes, valises and trunks, piled higher than her head, lashed in precarious balance by so many fingers of rope they seemed to have been caught in a fisherman's net.

"Miss Pettijohn," Baldwin opened up when the buckboard stopped. "You know very well —"

She interrupted, "I'm late, Lieutenant, and I'm dreadfully sorry," and smiled disarmingly blunting his reprimand. "I had trouble hiring a rig."

Baldwin had not seen her since the violent stage ride two days ago. Except to notify her by messenger when the wagon train was scheduled to depart, he had avoided further communication. She had, he noticed, changed from the modish gray traveling suit to a plain dress of some light blue material which clung tightly at her waist and shoulders. She wore another small hat, whose single violet flower struck him as both pitiable and brave. Excitement brushed color into her cheeks as she tilted a dainty pink parasol against the glare of the sun.

"Makes little difference this morning," he said, not ungraciously, and regarded the mountain of baggage. "Is it necessary to transport all that, Miss Pettijohn?"

"Why, yes," she said, showing an honest surprise. "It's all very important."

"You look overloaded to me. I must remind you that what won't go in your ambulance will have to be left behind."

She said quietly, "Lieutenant, I am a teacher and a missionary. I can be neither without my school and certain apothecary supplies."

He hesitated, having thought, instead, of foolish feminine frills and other unimportant accessories.

"Medicines — drugs, you say?"

"Yes. To be exact, one quart of paregoric. Half a pound of calomel. Two quarts of castor oil. One pint of camphor. If thee wants me to list the school supplies, I can." She looked up, concentrating. "Let's see —"

He held up a surrendering hand. "If you can load it on, all right. Otherwise, it doesn't go. Yours is the second ambulance," he indicated, a position he intended throughout the journey in order to keep an eye on her and possibly prevent her from meddling with the Indians. "Trooper Estep has been assigned as your driver."

"I thank thee," she said. Yet a sudden insight told him that considerable firmness reinforced her sweetness and light. She turned to look down the string of wagons, a radiance shining through her plainness. For a lengthening moment she seemed oblivious of all but the Indians, and Baldwin felt a dim alarm. Was she going to make an utter nuisance of herself?

A beaming boy trooper, gangling Private Estep, quick-stepped out to unload the baggage. But, first, he assisted her down.

While observing the transfer of baggage, Baldwin witnessed further remarkable devotion to duty when troopers Conklin and Daily, grinning like dolts, appeared suddenly to join the hot work. Miss Pettijohn smiled, thanking them with her melting eyes and her soft Texas voice.

A woman's presence, Baldwin thought, might prove tonic for morale. Conversely, she could create certain problems.

Soon afterward, he had the wagons in motion for the North Concho crossing.

Chapter 3

Behind them lay the red-clay banks of the muddy Colorado, crossed, surprisingly, without mishap, and somewhere ahead in that open world of rolling prairie and lonesome mesas, off north, was Fort Chadbourne. By summer the green vastness would turn to a parched-yellow brown, dry as dust, while on the horizon flickering mirages formed one quicksilver lake after another, always vanishing, always reappearing, constantly drifting and shifting in the wavering heat waves.

To Baldwin, riding in the first ambulance, the face of the land on the third day out from Fort Concho was a pleasant sight, flowered, fresh, alive with whistling quail, upland plover and whirring prairie chickens.

Since early morning, on both flanks, the train had been passing small bunches of buffaloes grazing the tufted grama grasses.

The Quahadas said they longed to hunt, being hungry for raw liver. Baldwin, replying wryly, had refused Hard Shirt's request to borrow a horse and kill meat for the entire train. Hunting could come later, if rations became low. Not when a feeling of order prevailed for the first time in the toiling column, a settling-down to traveling. Enough so that, judging from the screeching in his ears, Baldwin knew Rooney, as wagon-master, would be thinking of axle-greasing after supper.

When Baldwin halted at noon by a shallow creek, the descent of the Indians was not unlike the discharge of passengers after a wearisome locomotive ride. They dropped from their perches in waves, first the bronzed, eager boys, who went bounding nakedly around the wagons and off upon the flower-bright prairie; then the few bucks and the girls and women, until the last aged squaw came down. The Quahadas stretched and strayed to other wagons, their sonorous, flowing tongue blending with harness rattles and the sharp cries of drivers unhitching and driving teams to water.

Shortly, Baldwin noticed Miss Pettijohn start down the train, a ritual she observed each noon and evening. She passed slowly through the Indians, though never intruding, never speaking, never staring, displaying a sensitivity to Quahada propriety that continued to surprise him. She seemed like one of the Indians themselves, who almost always looked away when a white person approached and never spoke unless first addressed. She displayed to them a calm, warm face and an awareness of their presence, in it a liking which he could neither understand nor approve. If she ever ventured one meddlesome move among them, he knew he would stop her. Until she did, he permitted her to indulge her Quaker foolishness.

He lost her among the stirring figures and presently, when he noticed her again, she was returning, walking gracefully and not without causing troopers to pause in their duties.

It happened as he watched, as suddenly as the war party's lunge that afternoon on the Concho stage.

A small Indian girl waddled away, drawn by something on the betwitching prairie. Her mother called softly, unheeded, again sharply. The child tottered faster, attracted toward the musical jangling of a fractious, hot six-mule team, trotting so devilishly fast the slight Mexican driver handling the reins was being jerked along.

Rachel Pettijohn seemed to act on impulse. Lifting the hem of her long skirts, running, she caught up the child and stepped out of the team's path by the margin of a rod. There was an explosion in Spanish as the driver sawed on the reins. The little girl was wailing and Rachel was turning to take her to the Quahadas at the nearest wagon, when the mother rushed up. She snatched her child free and flung around. But not before Baldwin saw the stabbing look burning the dark dark Indian eyes.

Feeling fled across Miss Pettijohn's face, settled. She seemed stunned into immobility. She dropped her hands and walked in silence toward her ambulance. It was now difficult to decide, Baldwin thought, whether the experience had affected her or not. Her face was controlled. Yet he halfway expected her to hurry to the refuge of her wagon for a long cry.

Instead, seeing him, she walked on to where he stood.

"Lieutenant, why do they hate me?"

"You're white." He was being blunt and practical, not sparing her, not wishing to because she had to learn.

"But I wasn't hurting the child." She

shook her head and he saw her bewilderment. "The team . . ."

"I saw it. You saved that Indian kid from getting maimed or killed. To tell you what I think, Miss Pettijohn, I believe that Quahada squaw would rather have had her little girl hurt than for you to touch it."

That, he saw, she did not believe. Denial burst from her eyes and voice simultaneously. "Oh, no! No, she wouldn't. Thee's mistaken."

"I fear you don't understand Comanches," he said. "What you just experienced isn't unusual at all. You saw hate — pure Comanche hate for all white people, especially Texans."

"*All* white people? Surely only soldiers and Rangers, who kill them. I have heard of your McClellan Creek," she emphasized.

"In that case you should understand what I am trying to tell you. My company led the charge at McClellan Creek. We fought them, we scattered them. We killed some and they got a few troopers. Afterward, we brought them as prisoners to Fort Concho. Why? Because they'd been raiding the Texas settlements. Stealing stock. Taking women and children. Killing. I've never pretended the maudlin sympathy you Quakers espouse for Comanches and Kiowas. I never shall."

"They are no more than savage children, needing love and understanding."

"Children!" To him her ignorance was appalling and inexcusable. "Listen, I could tell you —" He chopped it off bitterly and swung his thinking in another direction. "They have a name for me. It's Stone Heart. Maybe I come by it right, with them."

She did not reply at once. She regarded him intently, seeming to find in him something he did not know about himself; with it an actual sympathy, which he resented.

"Mr. Baldwin," she said finally, in a tone so searching and exact and yet so soft he couldn't bring himself to stop her, "I believe it's thee who hates. Not the Quahadas."

Nearby a team of mules was getting out of hand. Rough voices ripped out. A white man cursed in practiced eloquence. These intruding sounds shattered his attention on her, yanking him back to the train and its constant demands. He said, controlled, "In the future, I suggest you let the Indians be, Miss Pettijohn. Don't bother them. Let them live their own way."

He touched his hat and heeled about,

aiming for the growing wrangle of hot-blooded Mexican mules fighting snarled harness. He paused after two quick strides, turned and asked, "Remember Private Fenwick — wounded riding escort for the Concho stage?" He waited purposely for her nod before saying, "He died the next evening."

He walked rapidly toward the source of confusion, his long cavalryman's legs stretching out, taking with him her startled dismay and regret. Fenwick's death had popped into his mind at that precise moment, and he had hurled it at her like a club. Cruelly, he saw; unfairly. And afterward the day, to this instant unfettered by delays, organized, in rhythm, turned completely unsatisfactory for him.

Stecker rode in from his post on the train's right flank and pretended to fill his canteen from a water barrel, meanwhile keeping a sharp lookout for Sergeant Rooney or Baldwin. After a bit, he jogged up the train to the Quaker girl's ambulance, his original destination, and let his mount idle along with the mules.

Rachel, sitting beside young Estep, saw him throw the muscular blond trooper an unwelcome look. Stecker grinned, his large mouth working. He flicked the brim of his hat to her and she nodded.

"How about swapping off for a while, Estep?" Stecker said.

"I've got my duty. You tend to yours."

"Aye, I have. Been out there in the hot sun every day, while you got it easy here drivin' the young lady." His tawny eyes on her were bold, moving up and down, estimating many things. She felt a sudden anger.

"You brought it on yourself," Estep corrected, "when you cussed out Corporal Higgins."

"Higgins deserved it. I was just holding up for an enlisted man's rights." Stecker leaned in; his voice roughed. "You've had this soft duty long enough, boy. The lady won't mind if we change off."

"You'll pick no fight with me." Estep's jaw muscles were quivering.

Stecker was watching down train. Seeing Rooney on horse-back, he shortened reins and murmured to Estep as he rode off, "Some evening after dark, eh, sonny boy?"

"Who is that man?" Rachel asked, sorry for Estep. His dread was evident.

Estep told her and explained, "He's been a ring fighter. A great many things, they say. Can whip any man in the company except Rooney." Estep nodded in absolute affirmation, more to himself than to her. "He'll get me some evening sure."

Late in the afternoon Baldwin heard a halting shout down the line of screeching wagons. He told his driver to stop and eased down, mounted his horse tied behind the ambulance and rode back. Right away he recognized the particular key of the broguish cussing as he headed for a knot of troopers standing around a sagging supply wagon, one rear wheel resembling the broken hindquarter of a crippled animal.

Sergeant Rooney was a sight to view and not to interrupt. He was surveying the damage, scarred hands on hips, bowed legs spread, jaw thrust out beyond his squat body. His normally brown-burned face was a flame red; sweat streaked it. He cussed in an unbroken flow of blasphemy remarkable for its descriptive passages and variety. Four troopers stood post-still beside the wagon.

Riding up unnoticed, Baldwin caught the tailend of "— son-ofabitch of a bloody mess! Blast it to heathen hell! Private Conklin! When ye saw the rear wheel was dishin' out, why didn't ye tell Private Daily to pull up? An' Daily! Me intelligence says a man's got feelin' in his rump even if he has no brains in his head. Couldn't ye tell, man — couldn't ye feel a mite of a quiver under yer seat — with one wheel wobblin' all over the domned prairie?" He slumped, overwhelmed by disgust, resting his left palm under jaw and cheek, contemplating the tumbled cases, crates and barrels marked U.S.A., containing hard bread, beans, flour, coffee, sugar and sides of bacon.

"All right, lads," Rooney said, resigned. "Conklin — you an' Daily have the honor of friskin' out to yonder ridge for two stout cedar saplin's. We'll keep one in reserve. Rest of ye start shiftin' half this mess to the next forage wagon." He glanced around. "Where's Van Horn, Ives?"

"Having a little trouble, Sergeant?" Baldwin spoke.

Rooney pivoted and his temper was rising again. His mouth fell when he saw Baldwin; for a moment he was speechless. "Trouble!" he repeated hoarsely. "Lieutenant, I wish ye'd look at that poor domned wheel. Even with a saplin' under the axle, this mangy wagon won't take three-quarters the load." He stepped to the intact front wheel and kicked its loose tire. "We got some soakin' to do, too. Felloes, spokes — bone dry."

Baldwin waited a bit before speaking, knowing that Rooney, who had never seen a copy of *Mahan's Civil Engineering*, always cooled down in short order and soon applied himself to common sense and resourcefulness. As a preliminary, he first had to relieve himself of pungent remarks suitable to the occasion, which was inevitably vexing.

"Think we can wobble into Fort Chadbourne without laying over a day at the next water hole?" Baldwin then asked.

"Maybe. Overnight soakin' will do if we make water by supper."

Rooney moved to Baldwin's stirrup, head cocked. His square face had smoothed. "Know what, Lieutenant? It ain't the wagon wheels or the heathens that give me the willies. It's the caliber o' some men we got along. That Stecker, Ives, Van Horn — the mighty airs they put on. Too good for the army, they think. There's work to be done, an' Van Horn is not in sight. Neither is Ives. Stecker has an excuse. He's out on the flank. I put him there so he can nurse his hate for mankind alone. If ye ask me, it's a bad influence they be on the rest. Particular, the young lads," he concluded darkly.

Riding back, Baldwin inspected his

flanks. He could see Daily and Conklin riding for the cedar-studded ridge. As usual, delay caused confusion. The Indian children, unmindful of the heat, were down and scampering, their wiry bodies glistening like rubbed brass in the hot sun. He paused to watch them, intent on their coltish actions, listening to their high, excited voices. One little girl was shaping tipis from cotton-wood leaves gathered on the Colorado. She had a way of twisting the ends together and leaving a smoke hole at the peak. When each lodge was finished, she placed it in the camp circle. Two boys, on hands and knees, were buffalo bulls in mock struggle for herd leadership, charging, head-tossing. Others ran in circles, darting in and out, astride phantom war ponies, uttering small yipping cries like coyotes. It occurred to Baldwin that he had never seen Indian parents spank their children as white people did: they seemed to control them without punishment.

A figure moved into the edge of his vision, and he found Miss Pettijohn watching him. Her lips formed a greeting, but he touched his hat and rode on up the train, disturbed by something he could not determine from here. Apparently, all flankers on the train's right had quit during the halt, leaving that side unprotected.

His anger erupted. He spurred between two wagons for a clearer look, and immediately made out movement on the prairie. A horseman riding furiously for butte-broken country. Baldwin hesitated, wanting the rider to be a trooper, in proper position, riding in that manner for a reason. Then he could tell it was an Indian by the way he rode and quirted what looked like cavalry horseflesh.

Shouting for the nearest troopers to follow, Baldwin jumped his horse out running.

Almost at once the Indian seemed aware of pursuit. He began picking the roughest footing and beating more speed out of his mount, a high-shouldered dun which Baldwin recognized as a platoon animal. Now and then the Indian, and Baldwin knew without doubt that he chased an Indian, would look back. Seeing Baldwin still after him, he would larrup the horse cruelly. Far back, two troopers tried to catch up.

Following hard, Baldwin entered a mesquite valley and splashed across a small stream bed and took the next slope in a horse-grunting rush, the Indian holding his lead, Baldwin hanging on. He lost sight of his man around the brow of a cedar-patched mesa. Rushing to that point moments afterward, he saw the Indian pause before a rocky ravine, blocked, and turn down slope from pursuit.

Baldwin thought he had the Indian half-boxed now. He fired a revolver shot overhead in warning.

The Indian's response, instead of reining in, was to quirt the suffering dun without mercy and, Comanche-fashion, flail bandy legs against flanks. Once again, the dun gathered lumbering speed.

Damn him!

Baldwin felt tempted to shoot to kill. He lined up the fleeing horseman, and hesitated. In the time it took to sight again, he changed his mind and spurred his mount, having cut some ten rods off the distance separating them. From the Indian's style of riding, low, ducked down, half-naked body like a fused part of the straining animal under him, Baldwin thought of a young buck's nimbleness. Except, his mind caught, late, there were no young men among the captives.

Both horses were getting winded. Baldwin, however, had the advantage of merely pursuing, whereas the Indian had to choose changing ways, and the land, broken through here, permitted no straight-away running. Baldwin was cutting down the margin. A little later he saw the troopers angling across, sandwiching the Indian in between.

Baldwin was surprised to see the Indian let up and strike a leisurely gait, appearing oblivious of the white men closing in on him. He gazed off. He seemed to discover a point of studied interest in the distance.

Baldwin clattered up first. He looked and felt a start of recognition that salted his raw anger. Hard Shirt was the Indian and he was pretending to halt in a friendly manner. Baldwin cut in front of him to grab the dun's bridle.

"Hunt buffurow," the Comanche said and gave the buffalo sign, raising a curved finger against the side of his head.

"Hunt buffalo, hell," Baldwin said. "You were running off to Quahada country."

"Hunt buffurow. Catchum meat. Damn betcha."

"Damn betcha no buffalo around here. None in sight." Disgusted weariness was beginning to dissipate Baldwin's anger, also the realization that argument was useless. Conversing with Hard Shirt always seemed to shift around to his own terms of

Plains Indian diplomacy, which meant ignoring salient points and repeating one stand over and over. "You're lying," Baldwin said, passing his forked fingers in front of his mouth. "And I thought you wouldn't talk to me in English? You understand it pretty good, don't you?"

"Plenty buffurow. Way off. Ingen hungry."

"You hunt buffalo — no gun, no bow, no spear?" Baldwin could taste the acid of his exasperation. He was going to order Hard Shirt ahead when a curious thought stayed the command. "Why didn't you halt when I fired? I could have killed you."

Hard Shirt's cruel warrior's mouth and arrogant eyes underwent a surprising transformation. For him it was a smile; to Baldwin it was distortion.

"Stone Heart" — and Baldwin caught the special use of his name, its summation of Quahada memory of defeat and captivity — "no shoot. Me" — the old man tapped his chest — "great friend of white man — of Stone Heart. Great warrior. Have many horses — many heap wives — strong juices in body." He reached out a greasy, flattering hand, his body brushing close to Baldwin, who got the musky reek of sweat and mesquite smoke. "Stone

61

Heart — big chief, too."

Baldwin pushed the hand aside. "We're going back to the wagons," he said, seeing the troopers come up on winded horses.

A greater fawning spread across the Comanche's features, across the cheeks as intricately wrinkled as if he had just swallowed an enormous dose of quinine. He pointed to Baldwin. "You send talk — my talk — to White Father — in Washingtah. Catchum? Stone Heart heap nice son-o'-bitch friend, huh?"

Baldwin's brusque motion forward ended the speech and a new understanding swept him. His problems were going to multiply in the days ahead because of this sly old Comanche, whose mind functioned along Stone Age lines. As Hard Shirt obeyed quietly, Baldwin had a closer look at the horse he rode.

"Looks like Van Horn's dun," a trooper said.

"It is," Baldwin confirmed.

Coming to the wagons later, Baldwin saw with satisfaction that Rooney was lashing a sapling under the axle and the disgorged supplies had been reloaded.

"Van Horn ever show up?" Baldwin asked.

Rooney paused, shaking a sweaty face. His knowing eyes sought the Comanche and the punished dun, piecing together the story. Just then, Hard Shirt dismounted on the far side, the Indian side, and the horse shied violently.

Baldwin said, "He almost got away. Little more head start and he'd made it clean. Wasn't a single flanker out there to stop him."

He swung away deliberately, riding down train. Along here the wagons carried only provisions. He rode to the rear of the first one and looked inside. Empty. Not that he expected to find Van Horn yet. Baldwin inspected other wagons without success and came to those hauling forage. In the last wagon he saw two boots and then the sprawled shape of a trooper reclining on sacks of shelled corn. Van Horn lay there, mouth open, sleeping. Or was he?

Baldwin rapped his knuckles on a boot. Van Horn stirred, but did not open his eyes.

"Van Horn!"

That jerked him up and Baldwin saw the bleary eyes open, blinking. "Get out," Baldwin ordered.

Van Horn dragged himself out. He was weaving as he rubbed his eyes and looked up. He had been drinking, but he wasn't as drunk as Baldwin had seen him on other occasions.

"Just taking a little *siesta*," Van Horn said in his blurred voice.

"Miss anything?"

"Miss —" Van Horn shuttled a vague look around. "What d'you mean?"

"Damnit, man, your mount!"

"My mount? Of . . . course. Seems that someone has purloined it. The farrier, perhaps, for shoeing?" There was pointed mockery in the last, making Baldwin wonder whether Van Horn was as drunk as he seemed. But, then, it wasn't easy to determine the man's actual sobriety, when he was continually on the disheveled side and often under the influence. Today, his hair was wild, his eyes inflamed, his sandy moustache untrimmed and food stained the open front of his rumpled blouse.

"All right, Van. What happened?"

Van Horn spread his hands and Baldwin saw the familiar emergence of persecution.

"I tell you I tied my horse to the tailgate and crawled inside for a nap." Van Horn pulled on his blouse and straightened to an exaggerated attention, chin lifted, back bowed, arms hiked out at the sides. "Now, sir, is that explanation enough?"

64

"It is not. You know you're responsible for your mount. Hard Shirt just tried to ride yours off to Quahada country. We caught him after one hell of a chase."

Van Horn shrugged. "What's one more louse-infested Indian?"

"Hard Shirt is not just one more Indian, whether we like it or not. He is a symbol of sorts of which you are well aware. What happens to him determines largely what the Fort Sill Comanches do. If he goes wild again, so do other bands. If he's killed en route, the army gets the blame and there's another outbreak. You were around headquarters too long not to savvy that. Which is why I can't understand what happened here."

"Are you implying that I gave him my horse? By God, are you!"

"You're saying it. Which, if I can prove, you'll stand court martial. Is that what actually happened?"

Van Horn, teetering, weaving, drew back in affront. "As one officer to another, I refuse to dignify that calumnious aspersion with an answer."

"You've already answered it, Van, and you're not as drunk as you pretend." Van Horn remained tight-lipped, haughtily erect, and Baldwin said, "By now every trooper in the escort knows it was your horse. This is just an instance. While I've had to ride that pokey ambulance with this damned leg, the command's gotten sloppier and more careless despite everything Rooney can do."

"Oh, yes, the great Rooney." Van Horn's upper lip curled. "Baldwin's Man Friday."

"Don't tempt me to get off this horse, Van. And, remember, Rooney's a damned sight better man than you. . . . So the foolishness stops here. Now. Effective immediately, you are without a mount until we reach Mountain Pass. You will report to Corporal of the Guard in command of the rear. You will march afoot — not ride — until further orders."

Van Horn's stagger was real. His liver-spotted face lost color, his moist mouth quivered. He came in one jerky step, looking up with suddenly sober eyes. "Will," he said, swallowing, and when he spoke again he was shrugging, conspirational, "you wouldn't do this to me. Why, we're old friends. Been through a lot together."

"I'm dead serious, Van. It stands."

"By God, sir, I shall appeal to General Sheridan himself —"

Baldwin would listen to no more. He

reined away, not liking what he had just done. Angry because Van Horn knew better; because there was no wish to grind down a man already on the bottom. Rather, Baldwin had been thinking of his small command, entirely on its own, its natural tendency to relax once away from the post and regular drills. A miscellaneous command made up of veterans and younger men, both of whom could be affected by the slovenly conduct of a former officer grown more slovenly. Letting Van Horn go unpunished would have only one result. Some had served under Van Horn, never a popular officer because of his overweening vanity. Dismounting a mutinous cavalryman was one drastic method of bringing him around, since he depended almost wholly on the strength and mobility of his mount. A horseless cavalryman was a demoralized one, generally a penitent one.

Rooney eyed him in mild surprise when informed of the order.

"Hell, I know it's severe," Baldwin snapped, dismounting. "That's not all." The other decision wasn't hasty; he had reached it soon after starting back with his runaway prisoner. "Hard Shirt is to be handcuffed and hobbled with chains. Day

67

and night. Inconvenient, I admit, when taking care of nature."

"Reckon just 'cuffs would do, Lieutenant?"

"The idea of leg irons is to prevent him from mounting."

"I know." Rooney stroked his bristly moustache, continuing his tactful, yet differing, stand. "Guess it's me advanced years or a softness in the head after wrestlin' too many mothers' boys an' rock-headed mules. I was just thinkin', ye know, how irons rub a man's hide in hot weather."

Baldwin pinned him a slanting look. "That? Or you think I'm taking it out on Hard Shirt because he's Comanche?"

"I was hopin' not."

"I'm not. And if that doesn't hold him, we will peg him down at night with rawhide."

Hard Shirt looked startled when the farrier approached with handcuffs, leg irons and short chain. Baldwin and Rooney followed. The Comanche wheeled swiftly, mouthing rapid-fire Indian at the sergeant, while his shifting eyes accused Baldwin.

"He wants to make a speech," Rooney announced lamely. "Says he will talk white man."

"Why?"

"He says we don't understand what this means."

Marching down to Fort Concho last autumn after the fight on McClellan Creek, Baldwin would have denied the request instantly. Today he felt a vague hesitation. Motioning the farrier to wait, he said, "He won't change my mind, but I will listen."

Rooney indicated so and Hard Shirt spoke in shrill, summoning Comanche, a camp crier's call. In moments the Quahadas were coming, forming a half-moon circle. Among them Baldwin noticed Miss Pettijohn. The Indians did not crowd around her; they left an open space where she stood, a reminder that she was out of place and white. Baldwin thought, "They don't seem to mind her as much as they did." Her status had progressed from outright hostility to a state of being ignored, which was something.

Hard Shirt stood aloof until everyone was quiet. He made Baldwin think of an imperious actor waiting for noisy theatergoers to take seats before he resumed a dramatic reading. At last, he was ready. His dark eyes never straying from Baldwin, he began, "Stone Heart . . . son-o'-bitch my great friend —"

Baldwin's face warmed. Beside him the

sergeant stiffened. Was Rooney, damn him, actually smothering a smile? Across, Miss Pettijohn continued to give the speaker undivided attention. Baldwin couldn't tell whether she was blushing or not, and decided not after three days in the train listening to troopers and teamsters address stock.

Hard Shirt said, "Long time — white man's friend — me." (They were back on that worn-out theme, Baldwin saw, as the wiveled features put on the fawning look.) "Me — *bueno* friend — all white men. Famous chief among my people. Steal many horses — mules. Me — many-heap brave — take many-heap scalps. When I say fight — ever'body fight. Damn betcha. All tribes other side Red River fight." (A derisive grin touched one corner of Baldwin's mouth. The devilish old murderer was claiming leadership of every band in the Nations.) "Let me go free — on prairie. I will stay across Red River. I will keep my warriors away from Texas. I will let *Tejanos* plow right down to river banks."

He paused, an orator's pause. He seemed to await the effect of his strong words on Baldwin, who stared back in silence.

"If Stone Heart holds me like squaw," the Comanche said. "Puts the iron things on me — will be like big spark on prairie. Make big fire — burn heap!"

He finished with a skyward, challenging sweep of his arms, confident and vainly pleased with himself.

Baldwin delayed his answer deliberately. "I don't trust you," he said after a while. "You will run away again. You will steal another horse. I will have to put the iron things on you."

Hard Shirt showed puzzlement. Here he had explained how important a chief he was, how strong and brave, how friendly, how smart he was stealing horses and mules. Surely the pony soldier chief was impressed!

Baldwin could see these things. He, in turn, assumed the insulting Comanche manner of ignoring and spoke, instead, to Rooney. "Well, he's had his blow. Better make him understand that *sonofabitch,* although it has a ringy sound, is not a term of endearment among white people."

"I've told him, Lieutenant. He still thinks it's the big medicine word for chief. Says the boys called him that last winter whenever they cleaned out the stables."

Shaking his head, Baldwin signaled the farrier, a beefy, impassive-faced man, who started forward again.

Before he could touch the Comanche, Miss Pettijohn left the watchful mass of Indians and stepped between them. Her sudden blocking motion stumped the farrier. She focused pleading eyes on Baldwin.

"This is cruel. He's an old man."

"Just what would you suggest for a runaway captive?" he said, employing sarcasm.

"Don't put him in irons."

"This man is a self-admitted murderer," Baldwin said, surprised at his calm, asking himself what more could possibly delay the train today and why he wasted time explaining the obvious. "He brags openly of having killed and scalped many Texas people, perhaps some of your relatives. Just a while ago he tried to escape. He is a government prisoner, in my custody. . . . You've interfered. Now step aside."

She didn't budge. "Thee's being unjust," she said, with feeling. "How can thee expect him to love thee if thee persists in mistreating him?"

"Smithy, handcuff that Indian!"

She was prepared to interfere again when Hard Shirt acted. His hands curved in the combing sign for Woman and for Pushing Away. Being a great warrior, he signed, he could not in honor permit a squaw — certainly no pale white one — to speak for him. So he would allow the pony soldiers to put out the iron rings on him and hold him like a mean mule.

He walked over to the farrier; arrogantly, he extended his arms. But when the handcuffs snapped around his wrists, he bent almost frightened eyes on them; and after the rivet heads on the leg irons were made fast, he took a tentative, hobbling step. The short chain stretched taut. He fell, all helpless.

Pity stirred in Baldwin, but he didn't move. Crossing his mind was the picture of a wild horse humbled to rope and bit for the first time.

It was Rooney and Miss Pettijohn who assisted Hard Shirt to his feet, and she whose censure stabbed Baldwin. He expected anger, which he found; but equally in her eyes, and unexpected, he saw disappointment before he ordered Rooney to move the wagons.

Chapter 4

Baldwin came awake to a throbbing pain. His thigh was aching again, interrupting sleep begun only an hour ago after inspecting the picket line. He rubbed the scarred-over place reminiscently and sat up on the leather-cushioned seats, made down into a full-length mattress in the Dougherty, pulled on his boots and climbed down from the ambulance.

The velvet night lay still and soft under a moon-pale sky, bright enough that he could read his pocket watch: three-thirty. When a man should be sleeping his soundest. A wind laced with grass scents bore out of the southwest. No matter how hot the days in west Texas, he thought, the nights had the compensation of coolness. Around him the Quahadas slept under and in their wagons. Two places down from his ambulance Miss Pettijohn's Dougherty sat between supply wagons in its new position, the side flaps rolled part way up to catch the night air. By four-thirty, with the first slash of pinkish dawn, the cooks would light buffalo-chip fires and the heavy quiet would be broken.

From here he could see the pattern of the white-topped encampment. Wagons, tongues pointed inward, corralled in a rectangle: that shape because, in event of attack, it allowed greater movement and afforded easier penning of stock without the confusion and whirlpool effect of the circle, a defensive tactic learned from Mackenzie. The troopers' shelter tents just outside. Next the mules and horses, then the sentries. Besides being staked out, sidelined and guarded, most of the animals wore chain-connected leather hobbles attached to picket ropes. Until just before dark the stock had been grazed away from the train, which assured grass near camp when moved in later. Baldwin's own mount was on iron picket pin and hobbles close to the ambulance.

In the stillness, while the mind lay tranquil and clear, a man could view himself with the candor of honest detachment. Therefore, he knew the leg had not been the entire cause for breaking his sleep. Persisting was the image of Hard Shirt, uncomprehending eyes staring down, stricken, on his imprisoned wrists. And Miss Pettijohn, the way she had looked at the last, in silence, as if she had been the one hurt. He wouldn't have minded her storming at him, releasing her feelings. But her silent reproach bothered him. Hadn't he stated sound reasons? Reviewing them again, he felt a renewed righteousness. How else could you handle an incorrigible Indian? He forced down the intrusion by thinking of tomorrow, when they should reach Fort Chadbourne.

There was little warning of what happened now while he lingered outside the ambulance. Somewhere beyond the picket line he heard a subtle variation of sound: an indistinct shuffling, or an odd murmur, growing as he wheeled in that direction, all his senses pounding and concentrating on that place. And quickly it became a drumming rush, the tide of many hoofs beating against the camp's perimeter.

"Hoo-kaaa — yaaa!"

A carbine's crisp report struck across the night. More yells broke. More shots. The camp erupted in an uproar.

"Get to your horses!"

Baldwin was shouting as he ran between the wagons for his own mount. He grabbed

76

down for the picket pin, but the horse was plunging and whistling and the pin and lariat looped away like a snapping snake. He lunged — and felt the iron bite across his hand, gone. He hauled up, probing the murky light. Out there, dimly, skirting the camp, he could see a rapidly moving blur and hear ringing bells and the terrifying rasp of dry rawhides being dragged behind racing ponies. Above the racket a new rumble reached him, unmistakable to a cavalryman. The horses and mules were stampeding.

"Stand by yer hawrses!" That was Rooney's anvil voice, carrying despite the turmoil.

Baldwin jerked and stood still, and glimpsed a plunging, snorting, kicking, crow-hopping mass. He could feel its terrible unleashed power as it rushed parallel with the wagons. He drew back when it swerved inward. He heard it strike the line of shelter tents with a whapping shock, tearing, ripping, and many metallic sounds and bangings as hoofs trampled and kicked coffee pots, canteens and pans. Some animals were down, thrown by their hobbles, tripped by stake ropes. Others ran free. He saw troopers in crouching runs, struggling to seize lariats. Men fell or were dragged. There was no letup.

Waving, shouting at the top of his lungs, Baldwin tried to turn the frenzy of animals. They tore on wildly, in walleyed terror. Lariats were popping, iron pins whistling. His revolver was in his hand and he didn't recall drawing. He fired over the tossing heads. He saw a wedge appear directly in front of him. The revolver snapped empty, the split closed. They swung toward him. He could not stop them.

At the last moment he dodged clear, toward the wagons.

As they plunged past, the enormous shock of their loss enveloped him. He tasted bitter frustration. It drove him pursuing, in rage, over the trembling earth, shouting challenging cries at the riders he knew were out there but could not see. He had the violent wish to come upon them. He ran until his legs twitched from weakness and his lungs burned and he was hacking in great gulps. He stopped to snatch up a loose lariat. His massive fury giving him strength, he jerked the horse off stride, was dragged down in turn and felt himself yanked over the dusty grass on chin and chest. The rope held and he fought to the end of it, to the halter and the quivering, terrified animal. Back through the greasy light he could see troopers in the same unequal struggle.

Finally, the yelling, the infuriating Comanche yelling, seemed farther away. . . .

It was a dejected and battered command to which Baldwin and the stock-gathering detail returned after dawn, pushing lamed, heads-down horses and mules. After ordering double rations for breakfast, he and Rooney took inventory of the train's losses.

"With what's been rounded up we can limp into Chadbourne by afternoon," Baldwin muttered, viewing the littered camp area over his steaming tin cup. Strong and satisfying as it was, the coffee had the undeniable scent of buffalo chips. It was remarkable how soon, on a march, everything took on that stink, from uniform to bedroll; and how, some mornings, you would swear the bacon had been fried in it. Baldwin spoke from a squat, too tired to stand. His rope-burned hands were swollen, his body stiff, bruised. He sipped the scalding brew, reflecting. "How far would you say we are from where Hard Shirt tried to get away?"

"Six-eight miles."

"It's got me wondering a little."

Rooney's blue eyes held a matching

speculation. "Think he figured a war party was out there?"

Baldwin nodded. "Except he was a day early."

"Lucky day, then. Saved yer hair."

Baldwin took another pull on his cup. "What happens next? What would a horse-thieving Comanche do after hitting us hard once?"

"Hit us again. Take what was missed the first time, an' free the captives."

"Even though it's evident we're headed in the direction of the reservation."

"Do they know we'll go on to Fort Sill, Lieutenant? Do they, now?"

"Hell, no," Baldwin agreed. "We could be escorting the Quahadas to Fort Griffin or Richardson."

"Me thinkin' is it wouldn't make any difference if they did know. No Comanche likes reservation salt pork. Rather run buffalo. Eat raw liver. Comanches love hawrses as much as life itself. That's one thing I know. They never get enough. Same as an Irishman loves his tonic."

Baldwin stood up and dashed coffee grounds from his cup. "We can expect harassment until we reach the settlements above Fort Belknap. But if they try again — and I almost hope they do — it won't be so easy next time. Hereafter, all stock goes inside the corral at night. . . . I know," Baldwin said, seeing Rooney's reaction, "it will make one hell of a commotion and a greater stink and it's impossible to hobble animals still. We won't get much sleep, but neither are we under the present circumstances. . . . Say you were in this war party, horse-stealing bunch. Where would you make your big try?"

"Mountain Pass," Rooney replied, not hesitating. "Where else?"

Chadbourne's designation as a fort seemed scarcely appropriate on the basis of appearance, and Baldwin doubted that any improvements had occurred since the captives last came through here. At that time a prairie dog village had possessed the parade ground, and the crude stockade had fallen down in places. He recalled Chadbourne's principal claim to pre-war note was as a way station on the now-defunct Butterfield Overland Mail Line and as a rendezvous for troops under Robert E. Lee, then a lieutenant-colonel, while chasing Comanches. Seeing the rabble of dilapidated buildings from afar, Baldwin could still question that two companies of cavalry occupied the post. But such was true and the flag on the staff said so again.

And shortly an entire company turned out from the fort and swung toward the train. Just beyond the ambulance, a young second lieutenant halted his men, rode up and saluted with parade-ground correctness. His voice came out startlingly formal:

"Sir, Captain Gilstrap presents his very best compliments and urges you to come to headquarters on an important matter as soon as you can disengage yourself. He suggests you bivouac down by the cool of the creek, our choice camping area. I am Lieutenant Lane, in charge of escort to your bivouac."

"Why . . . fine, Lieutenant," Baldwin said, unprepared, but going along with the formality. Chadbourne offered only one suitable camping ground and the train was already pointed there. Regarding "very best compliments" and "the cool of the creek," Baldwin could draw but two conclusions: Gilstrap's flair for ironical pomp and that arrival of any wagon train was a noteworthy occasion here, a welcome change in tedious routine. Only a kill-joy would not respond in measure. "Thank you. Lead off. And inform the captain that Lieutenant Baldwin appreciates the unlimited courtesy of Fort Chadbourne and will be paying his respects soon in person. . . . One question. How's the water?"

"Well, sir — about the same, if you know what I mean, sir? There's just a little more to Oak Creek this time of year."

Baldwin understood. He said, "Yes, we're fortunate to be passing through now instead of late summer, when you can taste the horse tracks." Chadbourne's notoriously poor water supply was another drawback, a source for diarrhea and bowel trouble. Even such corrective fluids as lime juice and brandy provided small relief.

Gaunt Captain Gilstrap, like his rundown fort, was little changed from the previous year. Perhaps more seedy-looking, sad moustache ends hanging at a more mournful angle, sandy hair more windblown; in all, a victim of that frontier malady known as post boredom, varied infrequently by patrol or escort duty or chases after those master horse and mule thieves of the Comanche and Kiowa nations, bent on testing Chadbourne's ramshackle security.

Gilstrap jackknifed out of his chair and was around his desk in two strides, crushing Baldwin's hand, starved for talk, "I'm glad to see you!" he cried and stepped back, performing a sweeping bow.

"Welcome to Brave Fort Chadbourne — Gateway to the Golden West. The Artesia of North America — Site of Oak Creek's Merciful Waters. Now tell me you can stay a week?"

"Pulling out early in the morning."

All at once Gilstrap's clowning evaporated and he motioned to a chair. "At ease. For God's sake at ease! I understand you came in a bit ganted, with a train load of Indians?"

Baldwin explained and added last night's raid without dwelling at length on the extent of his stock losses; they would come later, the time depending on Gilstrap's mood.

Gilstrap swore in sympathy and opened a drawer and brought forth two small glasses and a bottle of colorless liquor. "Positively the vilest mescal I have ever had the repugnance to drink, unless what you had here last year was worse. I suspect on good authority this was made in a goat shed and strained through some Mex trader's drawers." His mood swung upward again, brightening. He poured the glasses full. "Although I learned long ago you can't change this country, that doesn't mean I have to like it. Well, here's to Lieutenant Baldwin and his Traveling Troupe

84

of Bad Indian Actors."

"And to Captain Gilstrap, Defender of the West."

They drank. Gilstrap refilled and Baldwin, delaying, eyed his own glass. "Be grateful," he said, "that your mescal-peddling friend didn't use raw chicken to give it that golden yellow."

"Oh, I'm grateful. I drink it in preference to Oak Creek." A far-away look lodged in Gilstrap's reddish stare. "To think of the fine Kentucky whisky we used to get," he said reverently. "Would you believe it, I haven't had one bottle of honest-to-God bourbon since Christmas!" He drank with determination, Baldwin matching him, and filled the glasses again. "I trust you watched the prairie dog holes as you rode in. I'd hate for a fellow officer to break his neck in my front yard. Since last fall, we've given more ground. Just about a quarter of the parade left. I suppose headquarters is next."

"Have you tried poison?"

"Poison?" Gilstrap cocked a disparaging eye. "They either thrive on it or are too smart to eat it. At any rate, we are losing the siege, foot by foot, inch by inch, hole by hole." After another drink, he sat in silence and slowly a kind of glimmer, a secretive expression, filtered into his bony face. He leaned forward. "These dogs," he said, jabbing a long finger at Baldwin, "these squeaky little bastardly pups may be our salvation yet."

"How's that?" Baldwin said, seeing Gilstrap pause for the expected question.

"It's this way," said the captain, intrigued. "I'm amazed that I haven't thought of it before. Suits me if they undermine the entire post. Let them, I say. If they do, maybe brave old Fort Chadbourne will be abandoned to the little varmints." He grinned wickedly. "The possibility fascinates me, Baldwin. It does indeed. If the dogs win, I shall recommend moving the post south on Grape Creek."

"Because it's closer to Concho and the joys of Saint Angela?"

"Certainly not," Gilstrap replied, innocent-faced. "I was thinking of the drinking water."

Gilstrap dismissed his orderly for the afternoon and the conversation broadened, quickening along on divergent eddies from Fort Concho and its families, to the meaning of the 4th's abrupt shift to Fort Clark near the border; the many allurements of San Antonio, Baldwin's furlough, Indian raids, the continual lack of necessities and, most lamentable, decent drinking whisky in bad-water country.

"Speaking of needs," Baldwin began, sliding into the opening, "I am short thirty-three mules and nine cavalry mounts. You can see what that does to one platoon, besides short-teaming my wagons. Puts almost half of us aboard or walking."

"Can't you double up your Indians?"

"Captain, I have eight or more crowded to a wagon now."

"What are you doing with one damned platoon?"

"Only Mackenzie can answer that."

"One platoon" — Gilstrap's puzzlement was increasing — "escort duty like this — after what happened to you just a few years ago?" He seemed to catch himself, in apology. "Sorry. But unsatisfactory as your position is, it's complimentary to you, I think."

"Better say there was no one but me available to saddle it on."

Gilstrap snorted. "I can name you six officers he could have placed in charge. None of 'em worth a bale of hay. Men who've never done anything but grumble and hang back on a campaign." Sweat stood out on his prominent forehead. He spoke through moist lips, looking wise.

"He wanted you — game leg or not. That little furlough down to San Antone wasn't rest-up for the border. It was this Comanche captive business, was all the time. Rest-up for that."

Whether Gilstrap was right or not, he was straying from the immediate urgency, and Baldwin said, "At this moment, I am desperate for serviceable horses and mules."

"Afraid you'd come back to that." Gilstrap shook his head and considered the lowering bottle. "I can't spare them, Baldwin. Not even half that many. Honest. Above all, the damned mules. . . . We had visitors couple of weeks ago. One night. Naturally, we took after 'em with our customary dash. Yours truly leading the gallant pursuit. . . . Chased 'em a good fifty miles northeast. Never got a shot. Never brought back a hair. So you see —"

"What can you spare, Captain?"

Gilstrap looked pained. "Damnit all, Baldwin, you make me feel like a riverboat sharper. I want to oblige you. We're old friends. I want to, when actually I can't spare a single animal."

Baldwin argued on without success, a failure he hadn't expected after a bottle of mescal. Gilstrap would not bow unless moved by an exceptional event, and what it was to be Baldwin had no inkling.

His head was throbbing like a drum as he rode thoughtfully to camp through late afternoon heat. Rooney, he saw, had deployed the wagons as if the fort did not exist, in the usual rectangle. Good. Tonight the stock would go inside, for the nearness of the fort didn't assure protection against Comanche thievery. Riding on, he followed the creek for a distance, dismounted, removed blouse and shirt and scrubbed himself until his head cleared. As yet, he hadn't the key that would turn Gilstrap.

He ate his solitary supper. He sat a spell and felt the craving for an evening smoke. Searching for a cigar in his personal baggage, in the gloom of the ambulance, he came across two quarts of Kentucky whisky, his entire supply of spirits except one bottle of French brandy. He had packed them hurriedly at Concho, then forgotten them. He raised up and back. His mind settled, and seized unerringly. In another moment he had the whisky poked into a saddlebag.

When he located Rooney, he said, "Oblige me by taking this over to Captain Gilstrap. The usual compliments."

"If the lieutenant asks me," Rooney said wistfully, jogging the gurgling bag up and down, "he's got a world o' compliments right here."

It was that interval just before darkness fell, when gossamer light lingered, when every sound was softly magnified, when the grama-grassed earth seemed tired and the sky was windless. At sunset Baldwin had heard the solemn notes of Retreat straying out from the fort, plaintive and strange across the empty country. Around the wagons the clear voices of the children were audible to him in snatches of flowing Comanche. He had grown accustomed to their shrill unrestraint, to expect it about this hour. And to seeing the children, playing like coppery imps in the fading light. Hence, he sat on the tongue of the ambulance and smoked the last of his cigar.

"Mr. Baldwin."

He turned toward the soft Texas voice behind him, stood and inclined his head. "Evening, Miss Pettijohn."

"May I speak with thee?"

"Of course."

"I don't want to intrude."

"You aren't."

"I wasn't sure," she said, in frankness, still hesitating, "after the way thee's been avoiding me."

So he had — to the extent of moving her ambulance farther back in the train and shunning conversation with her, yet not realizing he had been obvious.

"You will have to agree," he said defensively, "there's been no time for parlor talk since Hard Shirt pulled his runaway and the Comanches took our stock." He found a camp chair for her, and as she stepped by him, he got the faint, clean scent of soap and woman. She was a little out of breath. Her unadorned yellow hair was damp and knotted on the back of her head as was her habit, though more loosely, less austere. The hard traveling, he thought, had changed her as it had everyone, even the Indians, and was still doing.

"Which is why I waited. I thought of so many things while I was walking."

"You went walking — alone?"

"Along the creek, yes. Was it wrong?"

Another suspicion broadened: the dampness of her hair, the obscure but delightful scent of her. "You also bathed in the creek — alone — didn't you?" Not allowing her opportunity to answer, he said gruffly, "Miss Pettijohn, you are deliberately inviting trouble for yourself. Never go off alone in Indian country! Never — in the name of common sense — go off down the creek alone and take a bath!" Building all the while as he tongue-lashed her was the intolerable picture of her in Oak Creek, alone, unaware, stark naked, her slender, white body glistening-wet while carnal Comanche eyes watched.

"How," she said coolly, "would thee suggest I take a bath? Send one of thy soldiers to watch for Indians? Well, if it will relieve thy mind, I wasn't alone. Three Indian women were there, too."

"I didn't know squaws *ever* bathed."

"Thee should be better informed about thy charges. One was Topah, Hard Shirt's wife."

"You mean one of his harem."

"I wasn't afraid."

"Neither were the two Schrieber family girls about a year ago, near Fredericksburg. Rangers found one alongside a trail. The other one — nobody knows what happened to her, but I can pretty well imagine."

"The poor things," Miss Pettijohn said, her concern sincere. "I was attending college then, in Pennsylvania."

"And that," he said, "prepared you for working with wild Indians?" He was purposely baiting her and belittling. He had no sympathy for her mission, which he believed impractical, ill-advised and maudlin. It seemed impossible to upset her, however, for she said, "Only up to a certain point. Beyond that lie the fruits of experience and maturity — and God's will for whatever happens, which I am willing to accept. We Friends believe in the rational approach: first make them literate and teach them skills. For the girls, domestic arts, cleanliness in the home, cooking and sewing. For the boys, stock raising and farming, harness and shoe-making and woodworking."

"Pretty dull substitutes for buffalo hunting, stealing and killing in Texas and Old Mexico."

"Mr. Baldwin," she said, a firm quality edging into her pleasant voice, "the buffalo will be gone in a few years. When that happens so will the raiding, and the Indian will need a new life to sustain him." She paused and folded her hands thoughtfully. She had been speaking with calm assurance. Now he sensed uncertainty. "There are many things I don't understand about Indians. Why, for example it's considered honorable to scalp their enemies and steal horses."

"That's the only way a Comanche can make a name for himself," Baldwin said.

"I still don't understand. And why — like Hard Shirt — they have more than one wife. Something ought to be done about that."

"Just why?"

"Because," she said, momentarily flustered, "because it's unChristian. It's primitive — lecherous. It isn't right."

He could not resist a laugh. "Are you referring to all his wives or just the three he has with him?"

She stood suddenly and stepped across, looking up at him. "Please don't ridicule me. I'm serious."

"Also misinformed, Miss Pettijohn. A while ago you said your Society of Friends believed in literacy and skills first. I suppose you meant before teaching them about the Bible? What you overlook is you are dealing with people who have no tribal religion, no dogma. Every Comanche is his own priest or prophet. They don't even sun dance like the Kiowas. And when you talk about cutting down Hard Shirt's wives, just remember he's too old to change from the old ways."

"Thee can do something. Thee's the commander here. Thee put him in irons, I believe," she stressed.

"You want me to tell him he'll have to

give up all but one of his wives? Is that it?"

"Yes."

"If I did, Hard Shirt and his wives would be very much amused, besides thinking I was crazy. They don't want to leave the prolific old tomcat. Fact is, Miss Pettijohn, if you are so set on making a Christian out of him, you'll have to take him just as he is — many wives, many scalps, everything heathen. Then go to work on him."

"It will take time," she admitted. "Thee forgets that we Friends are practical. At the present I am anxious about Topah. She is with child and will require care."

Baldwin felt distressed. "For the last time, will you let the Indians alone? They have medicine women. They don't want white midwives standing around. Furthermore, they don't need them." Watching her face, he became more impatient. Except for a tiny stiffening of the small chin, she gave no indication she disagreed. "It isn't unusual," he went on, "for a Comanche woman on the move to drop behind, give birth and rejoin her band after a few hours. I thought you knew that — or wasn't it in the particular books you read?"

"I've heard of such cases," she agreed, being precise and reasonable, which annoyed him. "However, it isn't necessary to read a book to learn that Comanche women aren't made of wood. They're human beings and they have souls and emotions, just like white women. I happen to know, from studying government reports on the Penateka band's residence in Texas before the War, that the death rate of Comanche women at childbirth is quite high. Being treated as they are like mere servants, carrying wood and water and tanning hides, the constant horseback riding — that doesn't produce healthy mothers or babies, Mr. Baldwin."

"You sound convincing," he said, surprised at her knowledge. "Go on."

"The Comanche people," she said, "aren't always the healthy race we whites think. Their diet is one-sided. Not enough, if any, vegetables. They are subject to pneumonia, rheumatism, broken bones, intestinal diseases, snake bites. In the past, white men brought cholera and smallpox among them — and uh certain diseases of the flesh which I shan't name," she finished resolutely.

He looked straight at her, hands on hips. "I can't share your concern. I have but one purpose: to see that these Indians reach Fort Sill safely. I'll discharge that duty. Other than that, I have no interest in them.

Which, I might add, is the same tender regard they have for you and me and any other white person."

"I don't believe thee," she said, shaking her head. "I have observed thee watching the Indian children. Listening to them."

"Which proves nothing, since they are always underfoot."

They drew closer, like combatants.

"But I understand now why thee hates Comanches," she said in a low voice, and paused. "I didn't before. . . . I want thee to know I am sorry for what happened to thy betrothed. I'm sorry — and I understand."

He was a long moment speaking. His mouth parted and closed. "Who told you this?"

"Sergeant Rooney. Don't blame him." Again her extraordinary frankness came through to him. "I asked him about thee. He told me. Thee has a wonderful friend in him."

"He is," Baldwin said. He wanted to feel anger, but could not. He wanted to feel that she was nosing into his personal life, but could not. "I guess it's time you do know. Might help you understand Indians, which you don't yet. I'm glad Rooney told you."

"He didn't say much and I had no right to ask."

"There isn't much to tell. You may as well hear it all. It will make clear my stand once and for all." His granite calm left him suddenly. He had to look past her face in order to speak with any degree of calm. "She — Marianne — left St. Louis three years ago this spring. We were to be married at Fort Richardson. Northeast of Fort Sill, in the Keechi Hills, young Comanches attacked the stage. There was a running, one-sided fight. It didn't last long. They killed the driver, wounded the guard. The stage turned over. . . . She died of a broken neck."

"Oh —" she said in a squeezed tone.

"They killed her as surely as if they had put a bullet through her. That, Miss Pettijohn, accounts chiefly for my unChristian attitude toward hell-raising Comanches and irresponsible Indians in general. The rest is obvious — I'm a cavalryman. To be truthful, I haven't tried to change my feelings. Nor do I have any desire to."

"I am so sorry," she said, her voice small, earnest.

He ignored the sentiment. When he resumed, his voice was as matter of fact as a dispatch.

"Those young bucks were on a revenge raid. For another horse thief killed in the

Fort Sill corrals. Eye for an eye. Any white man. Any white woman would do. So in a way I'm like your noble friend, Hard Shirt. My future has been decided by the past, and I'm too old to change."

She moved her head from side to side. "Three years is a long time to hate anyone."

"You're talking like a reformer now."

"No — a woman," she said, taking him by surprise. She held out her hand and he accepted it briefly, feeling its smallness, its firm strength. "Goodnight, Mr. Baldwin."

"Goodnight, Miss Pettijohn."

"Can't thee call me Rachel? We are friends, I hope."

"When we're at opposite ends?"

"We're not, really. We have the same purpose."

"I don't agree. Yours is to coddle a thankless race. A misplaced sympathy. Mine is duty alone."

"We are still friends."

"Until we disagree over punishing Indian horse thieves and murderers? Let's be honest, Miss Pettijohn. We have no common ground."

He saw the indecisive movement of her lips before she turned away. And watching her retreating figure, he had a sharp regret.

She had drawn him out of his darkness for a while. She had offered him the understanding of a warm and sensitive young woman. It was, he thought, like seeing a flower open. He took one step, hand extended in a gesture of retraction; but by then she was gone and the light was going fast from the sky.

Not until Baldwin's ambulance was well behind her did Rachel let her steps lag. She went ahead in deep reflection, unable to define the state of her feelings. She wasn't angry, she told herself. She wasn't hurt, she insisted, although his brusqueness, in effect, had been a dismissal. Why had he done so? Was it because, having let his guard drop just once, he felt he must raise it again, even higher, over such a very small thing as using a person's first name?

She could not recall his having a smile for her, and yet she had heard his laughter after a remark by Rooney. She remembered the half-light on his rather square face. His dark eyes were tired. The constant sun and riding had marked him. He was a bit on the rawboned side, if that was the proper term. His attitude, she decided, though unalterable and typically army, was no more so than that of the Texas cattlemen on the Concho stage. She was, she discovered, making excuses for his actions. Moreover, in strictest self-honesty, she knew that he had hurt her.

Coming to her ambulance, she was taken aback to see a trooper. She stopped. A big man whose grace was cat-like moved toward her.

"Evening, Miss."

She murmured in reply, thinking he would walk on. By now she recognized Estep's harasser. A deeper sense told her he had been waiting near the wagon.

"I'm going in," she said. "Goodnight."

Her words showed no effect on him.

"I'm Stecker," he said, as if she would decide to stay. He sent his boldness sweeping over her. "I've sailed places you'll never see. All over the world."

"Goodnight, Mr. Stecker," she said pointedly and started around to the side step of the ambulance.

He fell in beside her, saying, "I'll be drivin' you before long," and walked down the train.

Reveille and mess call had sounded at the fort, signaling another warm, clear day. Breakfast over, Baldwin's Indians, their lie-abed habits cultivated further after almost a year under army control, loitered about the wagons. Details were driving up the mules from morning graze and water. Baldwin glanced again to the fort and resumed his strolling inspection of the train, while delaying orders to harness up and form the column. He saw Sergeant Rooney coming, a question looming in his eyes.

"Wait a little longer," Baldwin said. "I hate to leave any wagons behind. Gilstrap knows we're rolling out this morning."

"Got all summer, Lieutenant."

"The Quahadas have. Time means nothing to an Indian. His belly's his time-piece. I propose to get them off our hands as soon as possible."

"Miss Pettijohn, too?"

Baldwin's brows flew up. "She means well," he said. "Just misguided."

"That she does." Rooney's enthusiasm was evident. "A hard worker she is, too. Every time I see her she's got a question. 'Sergeant, tell me now. About how many papooses to a family? What's the average, ye'd say? Sergeant, what is the Comanche word for love? Why do Comanches have so many wives? Do they all live in the same tipi? Is it true they marry sisters sometimes? Is it true brothers borrow wives?' "

"How," Baldwin said, smiling, "did you answer all that?"

Rooney's face had the discomfort of reliving the scene again. "I told her that as how me experience was limited to that of a fightin' man, she'd better ask the lieutenant."

"She's already started on me. I'm afraid you're meddling again."

"Well, sor — I figured it'd be a good idea if —"

A bugler was blowing Assembly.

Rooney, fumbling for words, seemed to welcome the interruption. He kept silent. They watched the fort. Long moments passed. Nobody left the fort. Baldwin gave a sigh of defeat.

"Time to get off our haunches. I'll begin by bequeathing my ambulance to Captain Gilstrap; that releases two mules for the wagons." They started going over details. Which wagons were in first-rate condition. Which loads would have to be shifted. The number of serviceable animals. Baldwin, in exasperation, broke off.

"I'm going over there for another jaw-to-jaw powwow with Gilstrap. We can't get along with a half-mounted outfit."

He was in the saddle when he heard braying and saw the bobbing heads of

103

mules stringing out from the fort — mules and horses. He rode halfway to the fort and halted to wait for the detail, which he saw was in charge of Lieutenant Lane.

"We're late," Lane called out in apology. "But here they are. Short of all you need. Hope they'll get you through."

"They will," Baldwin assured him. "And we're greatly obliged. There's extra stock waiting for us at Fort Griffin."

Baldwin would have turned as the first mules trotted past, but Lane's voice detained him.

"Captain Gilstrap's compliments," Lane said, in great correctness, and raised his eyes, which looked unusually wise for one his age in the proper handling of delicate matters. "He said to convey his best to you, sir. The very best! — as he is unable to see you off in person this morning, owing to an accumulation of certain long overdue duties."

Chapter 5

That day the train passed Pulpit Rock and Church Mountain in the glazy distance and marched over broken mesquite country to Bluff Creek. At the headquarters ambulance, Baldwin and Rooney stood talking while the yellow spires of cooking fires marked the rectangle's dimensions and hungering coffee smells spread over the cooling land.

"I want to reach Mountain Pass tomorrow with plenty of daylight left," Baldwin said. "We've been watched today."

"Most all day," Rooney confirmed. "Bloody heathens on our flanks. I don't like it."

"Corporal Higgins seemed to have more trouble than usual keeping the rear wagons closed up. What was wrong?"

"It's the poor condition o' the mules, Lieutenant. Still a heap boogered up from the raid."

Indians and troopers settled down earlier tonight, even the tireless children. Baldwin noticed that Miss Pettijohn, perhaps sensing the train's exhaustion, passed up her customary evening friendship stroll among the unresponsive Indians.

It was another clear night, infinite, mysterious — treacherous. Almost the bright-as-day glow of the great September moon to come, called the Comanche Moon by suffering Mexicans below the Rio Grande.

Private Estep lay inside his shelter tent, drawn up in a tension of dread. The prairie wind was rising, but just thinking of Stecker bathed his chest in cold sweat. Twice during the day, Stecker, in passing, had made the threatening sign: balled right fist against his left palm.

He dozed . . . was aroused to wakefulness by the heavy tread of boots crushing the short prairie grass. He raised up, head cocked, blood pounding. He heard the boots tramp up to the tent and halt. He heard whispers. He twitched as something scratched the tent wall.

"Boy — come out," a voice whispered.

"That you, Stecker?"

"Aye. Who else?"

"What do you want?"

"Don't you remember, sonny boy? You challenged me. I can't let that go by."

"I did not! Let me be!"

"Keep your goddamned voice down."

"I've no quarrel with you."

"Come out or I'll drag you out."

Estep held back, silent. "I'll talk to you," he said after a long pause, afraid not to obey. "But that's all." He pulled on boots, trousers and shirt and crawled out. Stecker towered over him, broad, menacing. Beside him, Estep saw Ives and he knew now that he was in for a beating.

"Let's go," Stecker hissed, grabbing his arm. Estep resisted in stiffening panic and Stecker's voice was like a grindstone in his ear. "You just cry out, boy. Just once. I'll kill you. We're goin' down the slope a ways."

Stecker's grip felt unbelievably strong. Ives seized Estep's other arm; they began walking him away from the bivouac. Estep thought of the picket line. At any moment a sentry would challenge. No more than a few steps and understanding crashed through. Ives — Ives was on guard duty here. No one was going to call out. His head rolled from side to side; his legs dragged. They seemed to walk a great distance.

When Stecker stopped, it was all at once. He spun Estep about, a swift, savage movement.

"Put up your hands. Try to be a man."

"I don't want to fight you." Estep's cracked voice contained a pathetic appeal. "There's no reason."

"You wouldn't swap places. You got uppity. Now take your licking, sonny boy."

Young Estep groped for words of reason, but could not find them and realized their futility if he had. Unwillingly, he lifted his knotted hands, and as he did some of his fear, just a little, left him. He stood motionless another moment, eyes wide, his face twisting, his breathing soggy in his throat, his heart pumping. He took a deep breath and rushed forward, swinging wildly, aching to tear at Stecker, kill him.

Past midnight, Baldwin, walking the outposts, found a sitting trooper slumped on his carbine. Baldwin seized the man's weapon. The sleeper snapped up and Baldwin recognized Ives.

"They could have walked right over you," Baldwin charged. "Report to Sergeant Rooney. You're under guard."

"Was nodding a little," Ives admitted, drowsy, unconcerned. "Not asleep, though. Knew it was you or Rooney on inspection. Why get up?"

"Go on," Baldwin said, driving his shriveling disgust after the man.

After another trooper had taken over the post, Baldwin completed his rounds and returned to bed. He was hardly asleep, it seemed, when a shot sprang him awake and sent his pulses jumping. Ramming into boots, snatching up revolver belt, he hurried out to find Rooney just ahead of him.

"Who fired that shot?" the sergeant demanded of two converging sentries.

"I did, sir." Private Daily stepped forward. "I saw something crawling right up to camp."

"Oh, ye did now, did ye?" Rooney's voice was crisply polite. "What did it look like — the devil himself, with feathers?"

"It was low to the ground, Sarge. Kind of gray. Looked sneaky. I challenged. He didn't answer, so I fired. He took off before I could tell just what it was."

"Oh, *he* took off. It was a *he,* was it?" Rooney groaned. "Ye poor, dumb jackass. Raised on a farm, too. Why, yer dear old grandmother would know that was nothin' but a coyote." The other trooper laughed. Rooney whirled on him. "Shut up,

Conklin. Least, Daily was awake. Now get the hell back to yer posts."

"Say, Daily," Conklin's mocking voiced carried as the pair separated. "What's the countersign if it's two coyotes?"

Noises fell away and the night became hushed again. Baldwin turned in once more, feeling an affection for these men which he doubted could ever be spoken. But the bums and drifters spoiled it. Tonight Ives had endangered the entire train.

The platoon formed woodenly, like sleep-walkers. Private Estep was the last to fall in. Hat brim pulled low, he stepped into the rear rank just as Sergeant Rooney barked the first name in the roster book. Afterward, Rooney about-faced and saluted Baldwin. "All present or accounted for, sor."

"Wait a minute," Baldwin said. It was five o'clock, with the rose-gray light unmasking the sluggish men before him in double file. Weariness and grumbling he expected as signs of normalcy in a trooper's hard existence. What bothered him this morning was the glum discontent he saw as a stain on some of their faces, attributable in part, he was certain, to three men. Over by the wagons, where the breakfast fires burned, the Indians watched in silent amusement. Their hostile eyes, their Comanche arrogance — spoke to him. *Why do the foolish pony soldiers bunch up every morning like buffalo calves to their mothers? Is Stone Heart afraid they will run off and leave him? Does he call them warriors?*

These insights surged across Baldwin's mind, after which he said, "Effective this date, Private Ives, for sleeping on guard duty, will be dismounted and march afoot." Ives, he noticed, looked straight ahead. "That's all, Sergeant," Baldwin said.

Rooney made an about-face and glanced again into his little book. "Advance guard today: Cawpril Pierce, Conklin an' Daily. Right-side flankers: Burch, Sullivan, Mueller. On the left: McGrew, Stecker, Hall. Cawpril Higgins, keep the rear wagons in tighter today. . . . Now, lads, let's get that coffee! Dismissed."

Estep broke ranks first, walking rapidly.

Rooney did not glance in the lieutenant's direction, but Baldwin had caught the scowling disagreement, the disappointment. It was Ives; in Rooney's judgment the assessment had been too light.

Baldwin limped over for breakfast and felt his own dissatisfaction, aware that certain forms of punishment adopted during the War for extreme cases had not been abolished. His immediate impulse had been to order Ives spreadeagled throughout the night on a wagon wheel, or tied up by the thumbs. Ives belonged to the contemptible crowd Baldwin remembered from the spring of '62. Conscripts, substitutes and bounty jumpers, their pockets jammed with money, herded into a vast camp for transportation to Grant's army, which was coming to grips with the Confederates in Mississippi. Later, they would desert, or, feigning illness, get into hospitals. Any ruse to avoid battle. Thieves, thugs, malingerers and cowards. Meanwhile, other men, brave, went up and died in their places.

Trouble was, Baldwin had found, the enforcement of discipline within the platoon circled back every time, unchanged, to one indisputable fact: every man was needed. Even Ives. Therefore, a commander chose an intricate course between too much and too little discipline without depleting the scant strength he had.

Baldwin looked up to avoid colliding with Van Horn, who barred his path.

"When do I get my mount back?"

Van Horn looked too small for his uniform; the walking had thinned him, reduced much of his bloat. In addition, it had deepened the creases in his angular face and heightened his bitterness. He stood slouched and resentful.

"At Mountain Pass. As I told you."

"No sooner?"

"No sooner — no later."

"You walk a man's legs off until you need him. Till you know he can do you some good."

"Yourself as well. You know what Mountain Pass is like."

Van Horn's reply was to slouch away in injured forbearance.

After seeing the advance canter off following breakfast, Baldwin, pursuing an established habit, trotted back down the line of jostling wagons. He touched his hat to Miss Pettijohn. He continued on — and glanced over his shoulder, arrested by the sight of Stecker at the reins.

"What happened to Estep?" Baldwin asked, pulling over.

Stecker motioned out, evasively, Baldwin thought. "We traded off for today."

"Who gave you the authority?"

"Nobody. Estep said he wanted to swap. I just obliged him." Stecker's scar-pitted face revealed exactly nothing. He gazed ahead, now and then flicking the reins.

Baldwin weighed such unusual consideration on Stecker's part and saw Rachel Pettijohn turn her head. High points of color flamed in her cheeks. Her large eyes were differing. She seemed on the verge of speaking, yet did not. It wasn't necessary, Baldwin saw.

He turned in some weariness to consider the head of the train, which was footing out in good time now. Vivid in his mind was the dread of Mountain Pass: narrow, its precipitous sides covered with stunted cedar and boulders, a place remembered for ambushes. Time was vital, if they got there before late afternoon. This matter involving Stecker and Estep was of minor import — was, if the slovenly image of morning roll-call hadn't lingered as a demonstration of many details which disturbed the train; in fact, threatened its survival in the face of serious trouble. No, he thought, *now*. An instinct he trusted, because it was old and tried and an honest one where troopers were concerned, prompted him to guide his mount in closer and order, "Pull up, Stecker."

He caught the man's startled expression as he spurred forward to halt the advance wagons. Swinging back, he sent a trooper to summon Estep in from the flank and ordered Stecker to step down.

Stecker's promptness was minimum. He took great pains in looping the reins around a brace, and his motions were deliberate as he descended. His bearing was a tight line between guarded insolence and passable obedience.

Baldwin missed none of this while waiting for Estep's arrival.

And when Estep rode in, Baldwin felt an instant shock and then a sweeping rage. The story was emblazoned in the almost unrecognizable face. In Estep's swollen mouth and cheeks, battered purple. One eye was closed, the other a slit out of which Estep had to peer by turning his head.

"I take it you didn't want to change places with Stecker?" Baldwin said, controlling his voice with will.

"I've nothing to say, sir." Estep's voice was toneless, unnatural. He averted his one seeing eye. The terrible beating had left his features puffed enormously, created a lopsided, mask-like appearance that kindled the anger.

"It's evident what happened," Baldwin said. "Whether you furnish the details or not. Are you sure you have nothing to say?"

"Yes, sir."

And Baldwin, beginning to understand, twisted about to Stecker. "What's your story?"

"Same as Estep's, Lieutenant."

Behind the heavy-lidded, watchful surliness, Baldwin saw something. So far, Estep was living up to trooper code. If he did not, he would suffer more fearful consequences later. All of which held a hoary repetition for Baldwin: the tableau of principals suddenly struck speechless when the company bully was exposed. Discovering it again cracked his patience. He felt the cheerless return of a knowledge that some things never change.

"Stecker," he said, "you're going into irons immediately after Mountain Pass —" He was dismounting, still directed by the old feeling of necessity. He had forgotten his leg. Now, when he turned, he felt it give under him.

Stecker was watching in rising astonishment.

"Meantime —" Baldwin said, letting his actions fill out his meaning. He was shedding hat, revolver belt and blouse, placing them on the thin grass. In the outer range of his vision, troopers were collecting, drawn by the smell of trouble, of violence. One grew to be Rooney, who sent him a warning look.

"Lieutenant," he said, sharply for him, "can't this be handled in another way?"

"We've tried other ways. . . . Stecker, remove your jacket."

Across, he saw Stecker's amazement dissolve into relishing confidence. Stecker's eagerness showed as he pitched his hat, snatched off belt and peeled his blouse and turned about, contempt playing along his broad lips. He rolled up his sleeves. A blue, tattooed crescent rippled on the lower muscles of his left forearm. Baldwin didn't miss the thick arms, the wide column of throat which was too large for the issue shirt. Stecker's shoulder muscles bunched in ropy folds and his deep chest stretched his shirt front without a wrinkle. He had no weaknesses, Baldwin saw, unless they might lie in the bulging belly and the flat-footed stance.

"Seldom an enlisted man gets the pleasure, Lieutenant," Stecker said and brought up his fists.

"You're fighting an enlisted man," Baldwin replied. He squared off, ready. "I came up through the ranks during the War. Don't forget it."

Each began circling in, tightening the distance between.

For all his heft, Stecker's swiftness was deceptive. He cut in quickly, arms swinging. Baldwin slipped aside and drove a fist to Stecker's mouth and felt his arm jarred to the elbow.

Stecker wheeled in pursuit. His face glistened, savage. He grinned maliciously. "Aye, you're fancy. Monsewer, the dancer."

Stecker pretended to repeat his bulling maneuver. Instead, he feinted and smashed through Baldwin's guard. Baldwin felt knuckles battering his chest and stomach. He fell back, hurt, unable to avoid favoring the leg, and revealing that weakness while trying to pace himself.

"Have to dance faster'n that, Lieutenant." Into Stecker's eyes came a bright awareness. He bulled straight on like a wild buffalo, head down, boots stomping.

Baldwin stood his ground, ducked a roundhouse swing, and hit him in the melon-belly. Stecker grunted. His face changed. He dropped his guard and Baldwin struck the pitted face twice. The blows seemed to infuriate and surprise Stecker, who gave a great snort and charged back. Baldwin, unable to move aside soon enough, was spun half around. He took another smash alongside his face that left his head humming. He snapped his knee upward in a feint at Stecker's crotch and as his man faded back, Baldwin punished the round belly and scarred features again. He could hear yelling as though far away. His heart was a drum beating high on his chest.

Stecker backed off for the first time. There was a gap between them. He was content to hack for wind. He dragged the back of one hand across his streaming mouth and glared at the blood smeared there. Violence poured into his face.

"Lieutenant, I've fooled long enough —"

Baldwin's mouth was dry. His wind was going. The weeks of inactivity telling. Already he had learned that he couldn't stand toe to toe with Stecker. His leg could not bear his full weight, a disability he no longer attempted to disguise. He had to decide this soon, if at all.

He saw Stecker tearing in — saw him check up abruptly. Stecker's boot hooked out in a wicked arc and Baldwin felt a numbing pain explode through his thigh. His cry mingled with those of the watching troopers as he all but went down, hobbling on one foot. Stecker piled in upon him, slugging, mauling, a wild noise in his throat. Baldwin beat off thumbs jabbing for his eyes. In self-defense he grabbed and locked Stecker's arms momentarily, taking a rib-hammering as he did. He felt rather than saw Stecker's doubled knee punching up and he slid clear, hobbling again, and absorbed a haymaker that dazed him. He saw blood on Stecker's flattened nose as Stecker twisted around to attack again.

Baldwin couldn't move fast enough. He knew that darkly as he paused, bent forward. Stecker was ramming ahead when Baldwin shifted weight to his sound foot and crashed the knee of his damaged leg into the fleshy mound of Stecker's belly. All Baldwin's strength rose behind the blow. He heard Stecker's agonized "uhhh!" before the collision knocked both men apart. He saw Stecker flung backward and then double over, clenching his bowels.

The sky was spinning in sickening fashion, as if it had come loose. The faces of the troopers swayed and rocked, blurred and returned slowly to clarity. Baldwin sat up and tasted the brine of his own blood. He saw Stecker jackknifed on the ground, both hands pressed against his lower middle. Astonishment still clung to his contorted face.

Baldwin strained up drunkenly. His head was reeling and he felt the first giant tappings of new bruises. He saw Stecker stir and fall back, unable to rise.

At that moment, Rooney stepped between them. His fighter's face was like flint. His decisive motion marked the fight's end.

But as the black fog cleared from his vision, Baldwin knew that he hadn't actually won. The differences between him and Stecker were still unresolved and would be renewed. He stared bitterly at Stecker, who had forced him to fight in a way he never had before, and then at the half-circle of troopers. An impression caught — unsure, that, perhaps, they approved, and he realized he wanted that powerfully. In the background he saw the impassive faces of the Quahadas, no doubt enjoying the unusual spectacle of two foolish white men trying to kill each other. Troopers and Indians, all pulled by the magnet of a bloody, crotch-kicking brawl.

"Stecker —" Baldwin said, pulling for wind. "You — report back to the flank — where Rooney assigned you this morning." He had to stop for breath. "Estep — continue as before. Driving Miss Pettijohn —" Seeing Ives and Van Horn he felt a twist of anger. "Rest of you — listen to me. I want something understood for the final time." His tortured lungs ached. He paused again. "Every man is expected to do his duty. . . . Maybe somebody doesn't intend to. Therefore — if there is — I invite him to come forward now and take his punishment."

He confronted the first man on his left. The trooper appeared startled. Baldwin singled out the next man and the next, sweeping his gaze across them. Ives stared back, expressionless. Van Horn exhibited his weary mockery no more. Baldwin came to the end. Nobody had stirred and he was inwardly relieved, for he could not stand without swaying.

A trooper started to leave. Baldwin's bellowed, "You're not dismissed!" froze the man.

"That's not all," Baldwin threw at them. "Remember this. You wouldn't be here, if I thought we couldn't make it on to Fort Sill. You will get there. Because, by God, I'm taking you through! . . . Dismissed."

He turned his back on them and hobbled across to his horse. "They have to believe in you," he thought, "so they won't doubt themselves later. Especially the young ones." For a time was coming soon.

He was picking up his blouse when Rooney came up quietly and murmured,

"The boys liked that, Lieutenant. Believe we got us the makin's of a decent platoon now. After Ives got off light this mornin', I was about to think ye'd turned soft. I was wrong." His warm, honest voice extended approval and apology.

"Forget it," Baldwin said roughly. "I'm softer than you think." His stomach rolled in nausea and his head throbbed to the crash of a thunderous headache. He had taken a fearful battering.

"Stecker got all he could handle today," Rooney said and his voice, though approving again, had the gravity of an older man's caution. "Got it his own style. Only way to fight his kind. . . . Just watch him, Lieutenant. Watch him like a hawk. Next time be ready to use a pistol."

Before Baldwin paused on the rim of the high tableland overlooking the broken country below, he could see the mirror flashes flickering back and forth, tremulous and quivering, in the brassy afternoon heat. He had noticed no Indians during the day, but that, of course, didn't mean none moved in the lonely vistas the eye could not reach. Thus, he felt no surprise on discovering them again, posted down there on both sides of the pass, high up, signaling arrogantly, in effect: *Get ready. The foolish pony soldiers are coming down.* Watching the quick flashes, Baldwin had the odd feeling of participating in a primitive game of chance in which his turn had come to make the next move.

Meanwhile, the advance detail of Corporal Pierce, Privates Conklin and Daily clattered in around him. No one spoke. Being old C Company men, they knew what to expect. Upon their sober, sunburned faces, Baldwin saw the reflection of his own thinking.

Looking off, he could see the land falling away and opening up to broken remnants of ridge and solitary buttes. Mountain Pass was a narrow gap or break which cut crookedly through the rugged mass guarding the vast plain beyond it. The "mountain" designation had first amused Baldwin because the landmark rose no higher than 250 feet as you approached from the northeast. But after winding through the passage and mounting the mesa-like land to the southwest, his opinion had undergone a radical reversal to one of respect. Height did not present much of an obstacle, true. Far more formidable were the shaggy slopes above the pass, which furnished cover for sniping, and the narrowness of the trail, which restricted movement to the floor of the pass itself. A command was exposed on both sides while traversing the mile-length opening. You could not dislodge Comanches from the rugged walls by charging them frontally on horseback; neither could you flank them. You had to root them out afoot or simply whip up your teams and dash for the other end. Judging from the reports of ambushed parties, the latter strategy had been the usual choice, sometimes fatally. As a grim reminder of past events, there was a small springfed stream in the gap and by it the debris of a stage station, burned long ago, and the naked monument of a stone chimney.

He sized up prospects through his glasses and spotted no pony movement, just the occasional, darting flashings. He studied them and the cedar-dark slopes and what he could make of the twisting passage-way, until he heard the rumble of the wagons arriving, when he saddled back with orders. He could feel his jaw setting in the familiar hard line, his voice was direct and he wasted no words.

"We'll rest half an hour. Tell Ives and Van Horn they can mount up now. Water all stock from the barrels. Won't be time in the pass. Have every trooper show he has fifty rounds."

After that, he assembled his noncoms on the shady side of his ambulance and discussed getting down into the gap and through it. Troopers afoot would carry chains and ropes to brake the heavier wagons' descent. Not a wagon started through until all were down. Thereupon, the train rolled forward together, not in sections.

Rooney was brushing his moustache when Baldwin finished, the sure sign of a question. "When everything's set, the lieutenant takes the detail on to the spring?"

"Yes. My thinking is to close up the wagons there again and go on. If we're blocked off for a while, we still have the water. They don't. From there we can make it through after dark if we have to."

"What's to stop a smart Indian from shootin' the lead mules? They could block the pass."

"If that happens," Baldwin said, "we cut out the crippled stock and get the hell on. Or leave the wagon at one side. We don't want any long jam-up and we can't have the train going ahead in pieces, strung out to be cut off."

Baldwin paused, seeing Van Horn come to the rear of the wagon.

"If you will pardon the interruption," Van Horn said, a superior twist to his mouth, "I should like to offer a suggestion."

"Make it," Baldwin took him up and wondered what grandiose strategy he was about to hear.

Van Horn strolled to the edge of the little group, pulling on his rumpled blouse and striving for an erectness that wasn't in him anymore.

"It is with great reticence that I enter into your discussion at all," he said, but the eager tone contradicted him. "My tactical suggestion is simple. I saw it employed with telling effect in the mountains of Tennessee, when I served as headquarters aide to General James H. Wilson, who, you may recall, put the finish to Forrest's madcap reputation as a cavalryman." He played his assurance upon them. "I hope you will pardon the personal reference."

At this point, Corporal Higgins' dour face betrayed the annoyed boredom of a listener anticipating a story already worn threadbare by repeated recitation.

"As you know," Van Horn said, laying an official stress on the words, "I'm as familiar with the topography of Mountain Pass as any officer in the regiment. I've been through it several times. As often as you have, Lieutenant. So my suggestion is this: after we descend into the pass with our wagons, why not dispatch ten or fifteen men — including myself — to flank one of the troublesome slopes? That would help clear one side, plus creating a lively diversion. While the enemy was thus involved, the wagon train could slip through, I should think."

He concluded on that self-liking note, his gaze traveling from Baldwin to the others and back again to Baldwin.

"Ten or fifteen men?" Baldwin said over. "Hell, it would take four times that many with any chance of driving them off, and I can't see stripping our wagons of defense."

The muscles in Van Horn's face went taut and his eyes darkened. "Since the stratagem just proposed didn't come from you, Baldwin, you prefer not to use it. Is that it?"

"We don't have the men, Van. That's why."

"Is it too adroit, perhaps, to conceive?"

The insufferable conceit of the man!

"Whipping that pass," said Baldwin, plain-spoken, "won't be done with trickery. It will have to be through organization and speed and keeping our heads. By staying together. Besides, if I sent fifteen men into those damned cedars and they got cut off — what then? We couldn't lift a hand to bring them in."

He got up, nettled by the purposeless argument. Van Horn, he felt, had tricked him into discussion only in order to rake up his own dubious background as an officer, knowing his plan would be rejected.

"Since I'm in command of the train," Baldwin said to him, alone, "I will assume full responsibility for what happens to it."

He stepped across to his horse, a silencing movement. Every man went to his except Van Horn, who was still nursing his displeasure when Baldwin turned toward the pass.

Chapter 6

They edged down the sloping trail one by one, in snarls of smoky dust, brake blocks rasping against rear-wheel iron tires and wagon tops swaying precariously and drivers "yaaahhing!" at wide-eyed mules become extra fractious by the fear of descent, and troopers straining on lariats. The captives resembled solemn brown owls peering from under the gray canvas. Their postures were rigid and their jet eyes wide, masking the fear inside them. Being plains Indians, they distrusted heights and manifestly so when traversed in the white man's trembling conveyances.

Rooney, horseback, prowled the high places like a nervous bug. If not giving orders, he was lending a hand when mules balked or cautioning or encouraging. Below, Baldwin had thrown out an advance guard and was lining up the wagons in position as they came jouncing down.

When the last one pulled up, he decided to let the train quiet briefly before taking the detail ahead to the spring. He studied the high flashes again; their frequency seemed faster and it was in his mind, knowing there was no other way around, how he had been visualizing and dreading the pass almost from the first appearance of Indians on the column's flanks. Riding forward, he became sensitive to small details. Down here, where the prairie wind could not reach, the air was hot and still. He noted the worn condition of the mules. Many still bore marks from the frightening night raid.

Overall, he could sense a new and nervous stillness. The teamsters had ceased shouting, pressed down by uncertainty before going under fire. What was going to happen? Would they get through? Everyone, including the captives, seemed to be watching the flashes for further portent. Some Indians stood beside their wagons, intent faces tilted upward. Hard Shirt sat beside the Mexican driver of his wagon and was likewise looking. Baldwin's bitterness spilled over as he watched him. The old murderer, he thought, would like to be up there this instant. He had been up there in the past and knew just how the game went.

Miss Pettijohn and Estep also eyed the fascination of the quicksilver flashes. She turned at the sound of his horse and Baldwin said, "Stay down when we start through. Estep, you see that she does. I'm giving the same order to the captives, Miss Pettijohn."

"Surely the Comanches above us won't shoot their own people?" He interpreted her small frown as meaning that she considered the order not only unnecessary, but illogical.

"Not intentionally," he said. "I'm simply trying to avoid having captives, wounded by stray lead, maybe slowing the train or causing undue commotion."

"Neither did it occur they might shoot at me," she said, her frown persisting.

He sat straighter in the saddle, and suddenly the wild stage ride to Fort Concho filled his mind. She still didn't know — she still didn't believe him!

"My God, Miss Pettijohn, come down to earth! You're a white woman. You're forgetting that and you're forgetting Fenwick."

"He was a soldier, Mr. Baldwin. I'm not." Color stung her face.

"You will do as I say. Take cover. If we can give them the idea your ambulance is occupied by Indians, so much the better." The stupidity of their argument at this time took hold. Still, out of his vexation he had to say last, "You might keep an extra petticoat handy, too."

Her instant, deeper flush and the uplift of her chin remained with him as he touched spurs and rode on where his eight-man detail, including Trumpeter Mueller, had drawn in for orders.

Conklin was talking. "I can't forget that little black-eyed girl back in Saint Angela."

"What girl, Conk?" Daily retorted. "The one whose husband goes to San Antone once a month?"

"Her baby sister," said the long-jawed Conklin. "The one with twins and no husband."

"Hell of a time to jaw about women," Corporal Pierce put in and bit off a chew.

"The best," Conklin differed. "Gets a man's mind off Comanches."

Baldwin was brief, knowing these men needed little telling. "Don't bunch up as we go in. Ride at intervals of about four paces. Column of twos. We'll fort up around the spring." Rooney joined them and Baldwin said, "We will signal you from the spring. When you hear the General call, come ahead."

"We'll be ready, Lieutenant. We're ready now."

They had, Baldwin saw, squeezed time down to the core. The sun was behind the broken knuckles of mesa. Everything had been said and nodded to. He led away. As his horse trotted off, he heard Conklin's jesting remark to Daily, "What do we do if we see a coyote?" Daily's reply was drowned in the rising clatter and curb-chain rattles and squeaking McClellans as the detail strung out down the pass.

Old sensations returned to punish Baldwin. As long as he could remember, every skirmish, every action, had been prefaced by dread and tension. It was now. His stomach felt dull and empty and his breathing was uneven. He kept his eyes flicking the brushy slopes to the winding ribbon of the trail. Sometimes he lost the mirror signals as the pass turned. But, always, the flashes were up there when he looked again. Continuous now, vibratory, tense. Pressure built up and a growing craving for action seized him. Across from him rode Corporal Pierce, then Conklin, the short Spencer carbine looking dwarfed in his gangling arms. Behind him Daily followed. Over his shoulder, Baldwin saw the others holding the intervals. He picked up the pace gradually, until the detail was fast-trotting.

Nothing happened. Except for the flashes there was no movement. We're not close enough, Baldwin thought. Not yet.

When the first shot came, his tautness dissolved and he experienced an enormous relief. He spurred into a gallop, with the troopers following hard. He and Pierce took them around a little bend and some fifty yards beyond, Baldwin caught the silvery smear of water and the dark debris of the stage station closeby.

Yells broke from the troopers' throats, for this meant cover and almost half the pass won. Bullets began to pelt the trail.

Not far from the spring Conklin reeled and grabbed saddle. Baldwin shouted, "Hang on!" He was holding up to work across when Daily swept forward, threw out an arm and steadied Conklin. So the two of them rushed on and the glimmer of cool water moved closer.

Baldwin had his struggle of uncertainty as they rode in and halted. He had counted on the Comanches not coming down to block the train's progress here, simply banking on plains Indians' aversion for infantry action and cramped terrain, which prevented their darting in and out.

Bullets raised spurs of dust as he legged across. He and Daily and Pierce eased Conklin down and carried him behind a sheltering rock. His mouth was open. The bellows of his chest rose and fell weakly. Daily removed his own blouse, folded it and with great gentleness slipped it under Conklin's head. Baldwin bent over, frowning at the gray shock in the trooper's face. He opened the bloody jacket and stared. Slowly, he pulled the front of the jacket back, and looked again into Conklin's face, carefully controlling his expression to hide what he knew from Conklin's wide-open gaze.

"Shortest ride I ever made, Lieutenant," Conklin said, in the laziest of voices. His eyes seemed to seek comfort from the crouched men.

"Train'll be up pretty quick," Baldwin assured him. "We'll put you on a soft bed." The shooting seemed to be heavier; then he realized the troopers were firing back. He tipped his canteen to Conklin's lips, left the wounded man's beside him and stepped to one side. He felt a tug on his arm and he looked into Daily's pleading face.

"What about him, Lieutenant?"

Baldwin looked back at Conklin and

walked farther on. Daily's voice got higher. "Is he gonna die?"

Baldwin stopped. Daily wasn't more than twenty and appeared younger, as if endowed with an everlasting boyishness. His face was smooth; he had an inquiring, open look. He and Conklin, a veteran ten years his senior, were opposites. The older man favored rough women. He liked his whisky. Daily was quiet, serious, likable. Yet a warm friendship existed between the two, as shown by their incessant bantering.

"You hustle over there," Baldwin ordered. "Stop some of the hell we're catching from those damned cedars!"

The unexpected command was like cold water thrown into Daily's astonished face, as Baldwin intended it to be. Daily started to anger, then the squeezed line of his mouth relaxed, he gave a jerking nod and took position.

After seeing the other men posted, Baldwin took note around him. Cedars and rocks along the base of the pass provided some cover. They could hold on until the wagons arrived, but not much longer. He felt a driving hurry. He called across to Mueller, "Sound the General," and watched Mueller raise his trumpet, and he heard the clear, throbbing notes of the cavalry bugle lift softly against the steep ribbing of the pass, lingering, strangely mellow and peaceful.

An uneasy waiting settled. Baldwin felt the grip of the clutching heat. Sweat dripped down his face and chest. The Comanches fired only when a trooper raised up, and the troopers, having still less to shoot at, fired back only now and then into the patches of powdersmoke. Sometimes a horse nickered shrilly.

A lull set in, and Baldwin sensed why. The Comanches waited for the train.

"Bunch of 'em up there," Pierce complained. "But damned if I can spot 'em."

"How's Conk?" Sullivan called.

"I'd better look again," said Daily, nearest the wounded man. His boots scraped rock and Baldwin saw him crawl behind Conklin's shelter. There was a drawn-out pause, and then Daily, in a voice hollowed by disbelief and shock, said back, "Boys — he's dead."

A greater quiet locked them in, posted around the hot rocks and pungent cedars.

"Goddamnit to hell," Pierce said, but there wasn't any irreverence.

Baldwin swore softly and wondered why he didn't hear wagons coming.

138

Presently a sound started, more like a low cry. It quivered higher and higher and caught, breaking on the terrible and convulsive gasping and choking of a man's heaving, tearless grief, of a man crying inside, unable to expel it softly as a woman cries. It ripped into Baldwin, it touched him. He leaned forward in an unseen gesture of help, and of helplessness. He stayed in that tense position until the racking quit, when he sank back.

So, therefore, he was taken by surprise when Daily shot up suddenly behind the rock and ran out, a wild cast to his face. He flung up his carbine and began firing into the dense scrub above, firing and flicking the loading lever and earing the hammer back as fast as he could, daring the Comanches to shoot.

Baldwin was in motion with the second shot, in a crouching run. He piled into Daily and knocked him down, and when Daily scrambled up for the loose carbine, Baldwin slammed him down again, rolling with him and hearing the strike of bullets on the rock's facing above them.

He pulled the boy behind a boulder and they lay heaped there for wind, Baldwin spreadeagled across him, locking his arms, like the victor in a wrestling match.

"You'll do Conklin no good dead," Baldwin gasped.

Daily said nothing.

"Listen to me!" Baldwin shook him. His voice was flat and driving, yet understanding. "Getting killed won't help Conklin," he said and saw a glimmer of sense come into Daily's eyes.

"I know — guess I went a little crazy," Daily said. He averted his face and Baldwin let him up.

"It's all right," Baldwin said.

"I dunno."

"You can't fight Indians that way and live."

"I know . . . but —" and the robbing grief flooded back into Daily's voice and eyes and Baldwin saw the struggle going on inside him. Daily pressed a hand to his mouth, so tightly the knuckles went white. He drew in a breath and heaved it out. His hand fell. "Guess I'm all right now, Lieutenant." His head was still hanging, but his voice sounded steady.

"Don't get your carbine till we mount up," Baldwin told him. He called to Pierce and Sullivan and the three of them lashed Conklin's body across his horse and tied it in the cedars.

They took positions again. The trumpet

signal seemed long ago to Baldwin, though from then through Daily's ordeal until now just a little time had passed. But it was punishment to wait and feel the unslackened hold of the oppressive heat while the afternoon burned away, measured by purple shadows banking along the pass.

Baldwin heard the running rumble and the axle-screeching of wagons before he saw the first movement up the trail. When he did, it was two troopers galloping in advance of the lead ambulance, its four mules running wickedly. Behind it the forward bows of the larger wagons materialized grayly through roiling dust.

Baldwin's "Mount up!" swept the detail to saddles and the troopers deployed hard against both sides of the pass for protection, ready to move out. There, waiting for the ambulance to lead in closer, he heard the gunfire break out.

He reined out onto the trail and then back, his attention nailed suddenly on the left-hand lead mule. It was laboring to keep up. It was —

He saw the animal falter badly and wobble and break, yet fighting to keep its head while jerking down its mate. They fell in a crashing tangle of snarled harness and chains and thrashing forefeet, followed by the thrown rear mules, and after them Baldwin saw the wagon, its back end flung sideways, skidding. It teetered far over, hesitated, and dropped slowly down, bouncing, rocked and settled on four wheels, shaking off dust like a disgruntled white hen, blocking the pass.

The detail rushed into the dusty confusion, springing out of saddles and plunging over to the wounded mule.

Distaste flattened Baldwin's lips. The mule was floundering to get up and could not. He hesitated; then he shot the animal in the head. Pierce was hacking the harness free. Four of them dragged the mule aside. Up the canyon men were shouting to halt the oncoming wagons. A stray Comanche bullet struck rock and ricocheted with a high metallic whining.

Private Daily clapped a hand to his chest and half turned, pain, bewilderment and appeal transforming his face. Baldwin lifted his voice, yelling, "Sullivan — Mueller — cover us!"

Pierce and McGrew and the trooper driver were struggling to raise the other lead mule.

Daily was down on one knee. Baldwin started across to him. He checked up, startled, and saw, with complete astonishment,

Hard Shirt hobbling fast around the ambulance, hands free. He was going straight for Sullivan, whose back was turned as he fired into the cedars.

Baldwin shouted in warning. He saw Hard Shirt's arm whip up and the sheen of a knife blade. Sullivan was caught flatfooted while pulling his attention from the slope. His sharp cry rose as he tried to dodge, as he took the slash across his thrown-up arm.

Baldwin ran over. He wrenched on the stringy-muscled arm and broke the grip on the knife and sent it spinning and hurled the Comanche to the ground. Sullivan, yelling, hurt, enraged, leaped in with carbine pointing, furious to kill. Baldwin knocked the barrel up. "Get back!" he bawled and saw the wounded man's uncomprehending stare. "Get Daily up — down to Miss Pettijohn's ambulance."

Sullivan's mouth was pinched. He held his arm. He didn't like the order, but he flung away.

Hard Shirt lay back-flat in the yellow dust, his lacerated wrists telling Baldwin the story. Hard Shirt made no attempt to rise; his puzzled black eyes said he didn't understand why a white man had spared his life. Now he waited to die. He would not beg.

Baldwin scorned him. Seeing that McGrew and Pierce had the battered mules up, he yelled, "By God, take him back — tie him up," and motioned the driver to hurry the ambulance on. Baldwin rushed for his horse. Bullets were hitting around again. He heard a yell of pain down the pass. Close at hand he breathed the hot scent of the troopers' covering fire. He swung up. The driver was lashing the mules into ragged motion. And in moments the train was stirring and unwinding, like a snake writhing under a hot sun, the ambulance jerking along unevenly behind its three tough mules. Ahead, Baldwin saw the rest of the detail leading the way.

He hung back to ascertain whether that momentum held all along the line. Pierce and McGrew, faces crimson in the stifling heat, came running to take their mounts from a horse-holder. Mueller had the reins of Conklin's burdened mount and was following after the other advance troopers. Sullivan was the last to mount; he held his arm against his belly.

Dust whipped up from the passing wagons, spreading a chalky haze over the pass. Rachel Pettijohn's ambulance loomed up. Estep was grimly at the reins, shouting, lashing. The side curtains were raised half-way. Under them, as if framed in a print, Baldwin saw the image of Rachel bent over young Daily, holding his head against her breasts. Her expression was troubled for him, her lips softly turned, giving, caring, maternal.

This was engraved across Baldwin's sight as they rushed by him, and as he found an unlooked-for beauty in her plain face.

The weaving wagons tore on into the thickening pall, the mules stretching out once more. Baldwin galloped his horse alongside, trying to watch forward and rear. They ran on in that pell-mell fashion. The big wheels created a grinding din on the rocky floor. And before long Baldwin saw the pass was gradually widening; in the distance an expanse of bright plain seemed to signal. That was when he realized they were actually through, that nothing could stop them again.

He reined off and halted then, not minding the dust rolling up from the lumbering wagons, feeling a strange dullness and blown-out relief.

A little later, when the last wagon had cleared the mouth of the gap, followed by Corporal Higgins' rear guard, he rode ahead to the Pettijohn ambulance. Estep was walking the sweaty mules. Baldwin leaned from the saddle and looked inside.

She sat as she had in the pass, still sheltering Daily's head against her body.

"We'll give you a hand soon as the train is out a bit," he said, unusually gentle.

She seemed to struggle upward for his meaning. She sat motionless, without complaint. She wore a dazed, yet calm, look. He saw the very slight shake of her head, the sudden directness of her gaze upon him. Her eyes, he noticed now, were glistening wet.

"He's gone," she said and Baldwin hardly heard above the crunch of the wheels. "He died back there in the pass. Just after we started."

Chapter 7

A lowering sun painted vermilion across the wide mesquite flat flanging off northeast, and the hot husking wind pelted reddish-gray grit against the oaken sideboards and loose canvas of the wagons. Curb chains rattled, overly distinct in the stillness. Horses stamped. A trooper coughed.

Baldwin, hat in hand, spoke the few simple, believing words and stepped back. At his low command Rooney, Pierce, McGrew and Higgins, the day's stain on their haggard faces, fired a single volley and Mueller's trumpet, as sweetly clear and plaintive as a mourning dove's call, sent Taps in long, slow wails over the dazzling emptiness. All this while the captives stayed in their wagons, showing the solemnity of brass-mounted images, watching, unmoving, yet curious. *Why don't the pony soldiers cry over their lost warriors? For they were brave. They rode at the front where only the brave ride. Why do the pony soldiers dig a hole in Grandmother Earth, when they could set the warriors upright in a high place to face the rising sun?*

As it ended, Baldwin turned and raked his gaze in their direction to let them know. And in return he received their unblinking, answering stares, which revealed nothing to him, no weakness, no regret that he could see and, because he was white, did not see. Facing about, he escorted Miss Pettijohn to her ambulance and made to go, when her voice held on to him.

"Thee blames them," she said.

He was let down, leaden with fatigue. He could see the marks of strain in her, in the stiffness of her, in her drawn face, left grave and subdued by danger and shock. He felt a distinct sympathy for her which he was at loss to express. And he hadn't the slightest wish to argue the point, for what she had said was true.

"Yes, I blame them," he answered.

"Thee made them captives. Thee brought them here, on this terrible journey. Yet thee blames them?"

"We're taking them back to the reservation where they belong," he replied and shifted one shoulder. But in speaking he had the feeling of being placed on the defensive and that his reasoning lacked conviction.

"It seems so cruel," she went on. "Punishing so many for the wrongs of a few. Why, Mr. Baldwin, do the innocent always have to suffer?"

He was baffled by her far-away and dispassionate expression, for his failing to find accusation of himself there. His mouth curled. "And who might the innocent be in this instance?"

"The Comanche children," she said, never hesitating. The mask of her weariness fell away. "Certainly they are innocent, I know that. Like the children of promise in the Old Testament."

"They will grow up hating like their elders," he said, unrelenting. "If they can't take it out on Texans, they will nourish that hate inside themselves to remember as long as they live. To pass on to their children and children's children."

"Not if we open our hearts as we ought, and love them. Truly love them. Show them."

"Love them?" he repeated, left incredulous. "Two troopers died this afternoon and you say that?" He eyed her squarely. "And your noble Hard Shirt. Your noble experiment. One of your savage, misunderstood children. Know what he did in the pass?"

She nodded somberly. "Estep said he cut Private Sullivan's arm."

"*Cut* is a generous term. He slipped his handcuffs. Came up with a knife. A handy one, I'm sure, kept by his numerous squaws. He tried to kill Sullivan when Sullivan's back was turned. In fact, he stabbed Sullivan. Fortunately, my trooper will recover."

"Thee left out one thing, Mr. Baldwin," she said, as serene as he was bitter. "How thee saved Hard Shirt's life."

"That!" he exclaimed. "I was merely protecting a prisoner. By rights, I should've let Sullivan shoot him on the spot. As it is, he will be around to plague me the duration of the march." She did not reply and he settled his lips together, disliking the drift of his speech. He felt the brush of shame; he had been harsh on her. And so, for him, he expressed a rare emotion. His gratefulness came out. "You gave Daily something today that none of us could. I thank you for that," he said and left her.

After this brief pause on the vast, hot face of the plain, Baldwin urged the train onward to wring several more miles from the tired teams before camping. By moonrise the bivouac lay in a stupor of exhausted sleep. It was the first evening Baldwin could recall not hearing the Quahada children or seeing their flitting shapes in the dusky light. Small sensations, small voices, small figures — yet he missed them. Somehow they dispelled the escort duty he detested.

Two exceptions to the usual order went into effect next morning. Stecker rode shackled in a wagon, and Hard Shirt was returned to closer-fitting handcuffs. He had lost his haughty arrogance, a comedown Baldwin had never considered possible. The old Quahada looked wistful and defeated; his eyes held an almost childish appeal. He sat hunched in his wagon, crowded among his wives and brood of jet-eyed children, staring out across the dancing heat. Sometimes he called attention to a familiar landmark. There, no doubt, he had killed buffalo or fought the hated *Tejanos* or rested his stolen horses and prisoners after a helling raid into Old Mexico. Once, Baldwin saw him raise his manacles, a movement suggesting an incongruous abject piety, and, two-handed, priest-like, gesture off where Castle Peak rose barren and fortress in appearance above the plain.

Fort Phantom Hill's lonely ruins beckoned some forty miles away, across mesquite valleys and broken hills showing signs of continued dryness. From experience Baldwin knew that spring in Texas could bring a glorious rebirth of nature. But in this section a dry spell had set in after the early rains, evidenced by the low creeks and the thin mesquite and grama grasses turning yellow and the earth like powder under grinding wagon wheels. Today there wasn't a cloud in the light blue sky. The train labored tiredly under the brazen sun.

During the noon halt Rachel strolled down the train, hoping her manner was open and receptive without any air of encroachment. Not an Indian spoke, a silence she anticipated. But now and then she noticed black eyes turning and trailing her. It was these tiny signs of progress, insignificant as they might seem, that sustained her. She felt grateful and encouraged. Equally, she knew she must guard against impatience. Until the train reached Fort Sill, she had to forget the school and content herself, first of all, to becoming acquainted with these shy, savage people by degrees, on their own terms.

She walked to the rear of the train and started back. It was then that she heard an outburst of voices in the now-familiar resonant Comanche. In them she sensed excitement and haste. A little way on, she saw Indian women collected outside Hard Shirt's wagon and an intuition told her the time had come for Topah's child, its arrival no doubt hastened by yesterday's excitement and the wild, lurching ride through the pass.

Walking on, she stood in silence behind the women, who were kneeling. She stood on tiptoe to look over them.

Topah lay on a blanket, her dark face composed. A medicine woman, old, gray, withered, her parchment face puckered by wrinkles, was massaging Topah's stomach with soft otter skins.

Rachel wondered why. As the massaging continued, she began to see and understand. She had read that otters like to slide down muddy banks; maybe, it was the medicine woman's reasoning that, through the otter power, the child would slide out; that the soft skins hurried the labor. But the birth, it appeared, was going to be prolonged. The child inside Topah was enormous, too large for the short, work-hardened mother.

As Rachel watched in sympathy, ignored, the medicine woman shrilled a command. Two women took Topah's shoulders and stood her up. Like that, they moved slow-footed toward a stand of green mesquites.

Rachel stifled her protest in time, as a number of facts made sense. There was no tipi or tent for Topah and not enough room in the wagon, which had become Hard Shirt's prison. Only the mesquites offered convenience for such an event. Rachel delayed no more. She returned to the ambulance and chose a clean, soft blanket. She hesitated over taking a bottle of castor oil and decided against it. Quahadas wouldn't take a white woman's medicine. A blanket would be a clear-cut expression of friendship, of her desire to help.

Nevertheless, doubt nagged her when she entered the mesquites. An attendant had scooped out a hole in the ground and was making a fire to heat stones and a bucket of water. She darted Rachel a look of raw unwelcome, but said nothing.

Rachel drew in on seeing Topah. She clenched a piece of rawhide between small, even teeth; strands of rawhide lashed her wrists to a low bough. She was pulling on the thongs while the otter woman, as Rachel now thought of her, rubbed with the skins. Another woman was exerting pressure around the patient's abdomen.

Rachel stood fascinated, affected by the practical primitiveness of what she was witnessing. Although Topah made no outcry, her straining arms and distorted face told Rachel the Comanche woman was fighting unbearable pain. Rachel could restrain herself no longer. Going across, she spread the blanket on the ground and indicated that Topah should be placed there.

Rachel saw the black stares rise, grate against her and drop. Then she was being ignored again. No one rose to cut Topah down and ease her to the bed. Preparations continued as before; it sank into Rachel that her help was not wanted. These women were practiced in the art of assisting at childbirth; furthermore, they were independent.

Rachel stepped aside. Minutes passed. She just watched, careful not to interfere.

Now, Topah was tugging harder; first one arm, then the other. A deep moan escaped her. Rachel's restraint broke. In sudden sympathy, she stepped across Topah's extended feet and reached out to ease the woman's anguish.

Instantly, Rachel heard smothered groans. She whipped her gaze around, startled to see the otter woman pressing a hand across her mouth. She shrilled accusing Comanche, she waved Rachel away. She began crying and gesturing violently. The other women's lamentations increased to a fierce chorus.

Rachel did not understand. She could only stare blankly, taut with puzzled concern. What had she done?

There wasn't time to learn because at that moment Topah spoke. She was writhing and tearing on the thongs, jerking, fighting. The otter woman called sharply, in an urgent tone.

Rachel found herself forgotten. She fought the panicky impulse to leave. She went no closer and yet a sense, a deep and intuitive sense of dread, held her rooted. She could not leave; she would not. She listened to Topah's jerky breathing and watched her flailing struggle and the women performing the ages-old tasks. Making the patient drink hot soup. Placing hot rocks against her back. Grasping her and invoking the otter's power.

How much better, Rachel thought, if the stoical Topah cried out and released her pain.

A long time seemed to have passed before Rachel heard Topah's half-stifled cry of mingled pain and relief. Rachel leaned in, glad for her. But in the following slow moments, a sinking realization reached deeper. Rachel stood rigid and afraid, a hand nervously at her throat. Something was wrong.

She knew beyond all doubt when the otter woman, quite suddenly, moaned and turned her shriveled face to the hot sky, arms groping upward, and uttered a screeching wail. It was a mourner's keening, throat-torn, tremulous, instinctive, terrible to hear, as only Indian women cry for their dead, a welling up from the savage past.

Rachel lowered her eyes, closed them. Topah's baby son was dead.

Baldwin saw the Indian women go purposely into the scraggly timber and recognized the cause. Recalling births which had occurred on the long ride from McClellan Creek last year, and anticipating a brief delay, he walked down train to observe Rooney's expert lashing of wet rawhide around a damaged axle.

He turned at the sudden wailing, understanding at once. The baby or the mother was dead; maybe both. His brows contracted over the consequences of more confusion and delay, and he heard the after-clatter of the noon meal die down, hushed. And, simultaneously, that single crying from the mesquites strengthened to a company of grieving voices. And next he heard the mourning catch here and there, swelling in volume as the Indians at the wagons took it up.

Baldwin was affected in spite of himself. The discord, rising and falling and rising, scattered an effect that was weird and depressive and aboriginal. With it, a wondering thought spoke to him. Did not the voices express the fear and loneliness of all races?

He watched the spiny trees. After a while, he noticed figures moving in there, and a familiar gray dress. He came to himself fast, in extreme annoyance. He made a chopping motion. When, by heaven, had she slipped out there? He hadn't seen her. She was, he felt certain, involved in this new crisis.

He paced that way and came under the low-growing branches, alerted by a difference in the tone of the wailing. These new sounds seemed short, angry, even vengeful. He hurried faster.

Rachel's back formed before his eyes. She stood slender and somewhat desperate, trying placating motions, floundering with her few inadequate Comanche words. Clamoring Indian women faced her, led by a wizened squaw whose vindictive shrieking was loudest. She was swinging a stick. She lashed Rachel across the shoulders. Rachel winced, but made no attempt to defend herself.

The Indian woman was ready to strike again when Baldwin shouted. She stopped, the stick poised, and he saw feeling jerk across her face. She feared him!

He pulled Rachel aside and motioned them back and saw, for the first time, the Indian woman lumped on the ground. The Indian women fell back and stopped, but continued to jabber abuse upon Rachel.

He made an accosting sign, twisting his outthrust hand left and right, meaning, "What do you want?"

Rachel spoke before they could answer. "Topah's baby died. I'm afraid they blame me."

His attention jumped from her to the women. "She —" his hands signed slowly, " — is good woman. Her heart — is on the ground. My heart — is on the ground."

Scornfully, the shriveled woman's stiff

hands flew in the throwing away sign. She shrieked, "Jesus woman — no *bueno!*" and worked her hands again.

As Baldwin saw the futility of trying to convince them, another perception crystallized. The old woman's fear: it gave him no pleasure now. Not that he hadn't noticed it other times — a darting look, a small gesture. But today the pronounced vividness in the withered face and the summation there was like nothing he had ever seen before. Truly, the Quahadas feared and hated Stone Heart.

He touched Rachel's arm and turned her. The screeching followed them. When beyond the insults, Baldwin stopped. "What happened?"

"I am trying to remember," she said. "I didn't touch her."

"*Something* happened."

Her face bore an intense concentration. "I watched them a little while. Pretty soon I walked over and spread my blanket out for Topah to have. She cried out, later. I wanted to help her. . . . I believe I stepped over her. That was when the otter woman shrieked at me."

"Otter woman?"

"The medicine woman. So I got no closer."

"Guess that was it," he said. "The stepping across. Some heathenish notion about a bad sign. Bad medicine."

"But they actually blame me. I know. I wonder if Topah does?"

She was upset and bewildered. He could not remember another instance when she had lost her poise. She seemed on the verge of tears; in fact, and a near panic was on him, she was crying softly and rubbing her eyes. He had intended to lecture her severely — but this! He was at loss what to do. He moved and stood over her, watching her face. From there it seemed instinctive to place an arm lightly around her shoulders.

"I don't know how many times I've warned you to stay away from the Indians," he said, reproving but not roaring. "You pay no attention. You go right back and run into trouble. You've got to remember certain things about Indians. They're wild, superstitious. Closer to nature than we are. They don't see life as we do." He was letting his thoughts run, impressing them. "How can you expect them to love white people when we are their bitterest enemies? Hasn't it occurred to you that old charlatan of a medicine woman needed to blame someone? Of course.

What better scapegoat than a despised white woman? . . . I'll send a gift down to Hard Shirt. Something to ease his noble heart." The feel of her under his arm had become a very real sensation. As he stepped clear, he wondered where his irritation had gone.

She ceased her sniffling and looked up. Her mouth relaxed; slowly her composure returned. "I thank thee for saying that. Except that doesn't change what they think."

"No. But you know you're not to blame." Seeing doubt cloud her face again, he made his voice rough. "If you're going to let one old squaw's superstitions buffalo you, think what it will be like on the reservation. If so, you'd better leave the train when we pass Fort Griffin. I will gladly furnish escort."

She elevated her chin. Behind her eyes he saw the flare of a powerful emotion. Her breathing quickened. Her breasts rose and fell. She searched his face. To his astonishment she seemed to find something which pleased her. And she had no anger.

"Lieutenant," she said, smiling, "today thee makes me feel we are on the same side."

His mouth fell and, finding no answer, he walked her toward the wagons, aware that she would continue to mingle with the Indians. Would, unless he set a guard over her.

Middle afternoon was upon them when Baldwin ordered night bivouac on Dead Man's Creek near Fort Phantom Hill, south of the junction of Elm Creek and the Clear Fork of the Brazos. Constant in his mind since struggling through Mountain Pass had been the fort's sweet-water spring. Here wagon wheels could be soaked again, hard-pushed teams rested and repairs made.

But as the train lumbered up, he could not escape the forbidding nature of the outpost, abandoned before the War. A small forest of smut-scarred chimneys, lonely and eerie even in afternoon light, towered over everything like gaunt tombstones. Over by the stone powder house was the post cemetery, filled with victims of Comanche skirmishes, snake bites, bad whisky and barrack brawls. Around lay rolling country dotted with mesquite, chaparral thickets and prickly pear. He never camped here that he did not think of the men who had served at this far-away post, of their monotonous duties and isolation.

Watering details took the teams away. Cooks went wood-hunting. Voices high, the Quahada children dashed around and away from the wagons — and stopped, staring mutely, in apprehension, on the ruins of the pony soldiers' houses. *A bad place. A spirit place.* They had almost forgotten their ride of a year ago. Hushed, they straggled back to the wagons; presently, Baldwin heard the subdued murmur of their voices rising again. In time the camp quieted; it seemed to doze as the afternoon passed.

His first intimation of trouble was the crash of Rooney's brogue, always more marked when angry, and it was so now. Close afterward came the tramp of boots in quick-step. Baldwin, recognizing these familiar signals, got down from the ambulance and was waiting when the sergeant appeared, Ives in advance.

"Hate to break up yer siesta, Lieutenant," Rooney said. "Caught Ives, here, among the heathen bucks. Not only was a game o' chance goin' on, but Ives was cheatin'."

Ives arched up in protest. "I didn't cheat, sir," he said, full of innocence. "The Indians are just poor losers. It was the bullet game. They couldn't guess what hand I had it in. They thought they'd fool me — I took 'em at their own game, Lieutenant. I cleaned them out good, too."

"You know the order," Baldwin said. "No mixing with the captives."

"They invited me, Lieutenant. I didn't make the first move. Everybody was resting. I didn't see how it'd do any harm." He shrugged and it steadied in Baldwin that Ives' smooth tongue could make almost any act sound excusable. Ives played his innocence on Rooney. "Been all right, maybe, if the Indians had won."

Rooney seemed to lay an iron grip on his temper. He worked his lips and cocked his head and rolled his eyes skyward. "Ives," he said, "it's enough to make a saint cuss, the way ye've been mistreated in this outfit. Me heart is heavy." As suddenly, his voice changed back to the old bark. "Besides gamblin', which is against orders; besides gettin' chummy with the heathens, which is against orders — ye failed to tell the lieutenant just how ye happened to win their blankets an' trinkets."

"I told him."

"The heathens claim ye hid the bullet on yer person. When they complained, ye wouldn't open both hands at the same time. That's what caused the uproar. Ye didn't tell that to the lieutenant."

Ives stirred his soft body. He shrugged. His cat's grin formed. "I deny that, sir. It's Comanche word against a trooper's."

Baldwin studied the bland, quick-silver face. He said, "If the Indians don't make trouble, you find a way," and came to his decision. "You will return the Indians' articles immediately. Beginning tonight, you will do extra guard duty for a week. . . . Sergeant, post Ives as far as you can from the Indians' wagons. Dismissed."

Baldwin was prepared for protest, for at least one rebuttal of innocence. Instead, Ives seemed to accept the order ungrudgingly as he saluted and about-faced away.

Rooney stared after him, curious, distrusting. "Now what's so domned cheerful about extra duty? Answer me that. Why, it's like he cheated the heathens just so I'd catch him."

At twilight Baldwin saw Rachel walk past the old powder house toward the rock stairway leading down to the cool spring. She was an unusual young woman, he thought, and a restless one. One with a concealed prettiness of which she was unaware. His mind slipped back to the race down the dusty pass and what he had glimpsed in her. As if he had stumbled onto a secret place — remote, sheltered, fair — and, for one flash of time, gazed into the deep, clear pool of the heart and soul. An intensely personal thing. Therefore, he hadn't referred to it, nor would he. Would she ever, in her self-sufficiency, have need of a man? The love she talked about was different. A compound of human concern — teaching, understanding, compassion, non-violence. Giving. Demanding nothing. It required suffering and steadfastness and turning the cheek to these savage people, who despised her because her skin was enemy white. He remembered the medicine woman (actually, he thought of her as a malevolent old witch of the mesquites) striking Rachel and Rachel flinching but accepting the blow, not striking back. That memory still angered him. But Rachel, he knew, would follow the same non-resistance again.

And so, knowing her this well, he could just about mark her movements. She would wander up and down the wagons and around camp, alone, unafraid, not seeming to mind a solitude that would frighten most women. He did not call her back now or caution her. He had other times; on every occasion, she had managed to evade his order without appearing to do so. It was her will, her way. And yet, he thought, with all that, she was still a woman made for love.

Night let down and the paleness of the naked spires held on dimly, and campfires threw leaping cones of golden light across the bowed canvas and etched the enduring faces of the captives.

Baldwin passed Hard Shirt's fire and received not even an uplifted glance of notice. It was his custom to inspect the outposts about now. He walked past the rear wagons to the sentry there, beginning a tour that would take him completely around the encampment. A full moon spread a mist of silver over the pale facing of the ruined shafts. Hearing the singing cries of scattered coyotes, high-wailing, drawn-out, he recalled an old frontier belief: "Comanches are seldom near when coyotes are close." He decided there was something to that; for example, he hadn't heard coyotes the night the Comanches ran off the train's stock.

He passed the two posts along the creek and found them in order. He came to Estep, the first sentry beyond the creek, spoke to him, and next reached the vicinity of the post farthest among the chimneys.

Nearby he saw Ives strolling back and forth, assigned the loneliest place of all tonight. He was, however, carrying out his duties in an alert manner, giving Baldwin cause for reflection as he approached.

Ives pivoted smartly and challenged. Baldwin gave the countersign and was passing on when Ives spoke.

"Lieutenant, could you come back here after you finish your rounds?"

"Something wrong?"

"Well — I don't know, sir," Ives said, puzzlement and an unsteadiness combined in his normally cocksure voice.

Baldwin crossed back, somehow unable to share the same alarm. Ives was watching the dim silhouettes of the other chimney spires.

"I can't make it out, sir. Something's been moving out there off and on for ten minutes."

"Did you challenge?"

"No, sir. It never comes in close enough."

"Probably a coyote," Baldwin said, thinking of Private Daily's experience on Bluff Creek.

"But, sir, it's not low to the ground the way a coyote moves. It's taller."

"You don't believe in ghosts, do you, Ives?" Baldwin replied skeptically.

"It's no ghost, sir."

"Whatever it is, why haven't you shot at it?"

"Didn't want to rouse the camp unless necessary."

"You should have investigated."

Ives' voice, while disagreeing, was respectful. "Sergeant Rooney made it plain I was not to leave my post, sir."

"An order like that never means you're not to act within the bounds of reason."

Running through Baldwin's mind was a curious, suspended judgment regarding Ives' conduct. It was most proper, most unusual for a man who had slept on his carbine some nights ago, who had spent a good part of his time in the Fort Concho guardhouse for dodging duty. But tonight it was "sir" this and "sir" that and strict attention to small details. Trouble-makers didn't about-face that fast, not between the short space of cheating Indian prisoners in violation of orders and going on guard duty.

"Then I hereby give you authority to leave your post," Baldwin said. "We'll both take a look."

"Yes, sir," said Ives, hesitating.

"Lead off."

"If you say so, Lieutenant, sir."

Which ruffled Baldwin deeper as he drew his revolver and followed.

Ives displayed commendable caution. He moved with a stalking slowness, like an alert skirmisher. After about four rods, he halted and gazed around and advanced again. Baldwin saw nothing wrong and heard nothing but the paced crunch of their boots. Moon-wash provided fairly distinct light, except where the tall chimneys framed long black shadows. As Baldwin moved ahead, he lost the camp noises entirely.

Ives paused again, swinging his gaze. "Right about there, sir," he whispered and pointed his carbine.

"Let's go over there," said Baldwin, though seeing no change in the gloom.

Ives obeyed slowly. He kept turning his head and was soon delaying once more, a dawdling that rubbed Baldwin's impatience. Not a sign of movement had he seen. Nothing suspicious whatever. No sounds.

The continued emptiness, the stillness, the mounting vagueness, the sensation that he was looking for something nonexistent — Baldwin didn't know what prompted him to pause, then go on. He saw Ives stop, saw him drift back several steps.

A wrongness filled Baldwin. Ives was moving, now motionless beside him. Baldwin halted with slow care and felt a sharper unease; it surged suddenly, racing through him. And he wheeled toward Ives, but Ives, quickly, was behind him and he felt a jab in his back.

"Drop the pistol, Lieutenant."

Baldwin made a startled sound. "Ives — what the hell's got into you?"

"Drop it, *Lieutenant, sir,* or I'll blow your goddamned head off, *sir.*" Ives' voice was deadly flat.

Baldwin let the weapon slide from his right hand.

"Move up a step."

"Why don't you pick it up now?" Baldwin said softly and fought the edgy impulse to risk a turning dive. It was still with him when he felt a bite of pain as Ives rammed the carbine barrel high against his back, propelling him forward. When Baldwin glanced back, Ives was straightening up with the revolver.

"Stop right there," Ives said. "Don't call out." He gave a just-audible whistle.

Boots rasped gravel. Baldwin saw a figure leave the thicket blackness around a chimney. A man whom the peeling light outlined menacingly. A stocky man, wide

172

of body. Baldwin's throat tightened as he recognized Stecker and saw the revolver bulking in Stecker's hand.

"Aye, you pulled it off slick, Ives. Slick as a whistle. Nothin' dumber than a son-of-a-bitchin' lieutenant. How you like it, Shoulder Straps?"

"Put down those pistols," Baldwin bluffed. "Both of you. Start for camp."

"Listen to old Shoulder Straps jaw," Stecker mocked, jutting his face within inches of Baldwin's, and Baldwin could feel the destruction in the man so strongly it was like a smell around them. "Can't you understand yet? You're not back at Concho with the whole regiment behind you. Not any more you ain't! You're out in big country where a man does as he pleases."

Baldwin shifted his gaze from Stecker to Ives, in self-reproof. He had walked into one of the oldest traps ever set for man, the pretending-to-look-for-something ruse; as careless and naive as the schoolboy told to look up into the tree for the little bird that wasn't there and having his opponent fell him.

"How did you get loose?" he demanded of Stecker.

"Mean you haven't figured it out?"

Stecker jeered maliciously and hooked a thumb toward Ives. "He managed it — this evening — 'fore he went on guard. Even staked out our horses while he was on water detail. We planned this a long time back, Lieutenant. Fort Griffin ain't far. Th' hide oufits are lookin' for men."

"Why tell me?"

" 'Cause we're gonna take you down the creek. Finish you 'fore we ride out."

"You'll be hunted down."

"Shut up!" Ives swore at him. "Stecker, you talk too damn much. Come on. Let's get a move on before somebody comes. Estep's on the next post. . . . Lieutenant," he snarled acidly, "you better make sure we reach those horses. If we're challenged, you say it's all right. If you don't, you're dead that much quicker."

Baldwin was pushed forward. Ives' carbine prodded his back and he could hear Stecker's heavier step close behind on the other flank. Ives pointed them up creek, angling away from the nearest outpost, which was Estep's. At this distance Baldwin couldn't make out Estep, but he knew about where the post was. He turned his head, continuing to search the dimness for Estep's pacing shape. He couldn't find it; he dragged step.

"Move!" Ives hissed and jabbed.

Baldwin was straining for a way out. He thought of calling Estep's name, and realized Estep couldn't come fast enough. He forced the notion down. He saw the dark wall of the creek's trees. Once there he had less chance. Again he rose to the point of decision, and again it slipped away when Ives drove the carbine into his flesh.

Desperation became thick and dry in Baldwin's throat as they entered the timber. His heart was pounding. Here, Ives took the lead and Stecker fell in behind, keeping the nose of his revolver hard against Baldwin's spine. For what seemed a long time to Baldwin they tramped through the deep dark of the timber. Once Stecker hissed a warning to Ives, who pulled up. Baldwin listened with them, his wild hope soaring again. The silence behind them merely congealed.

Ives started on, faster. When Baldwin slowed, Stecker rammed the revolver harder. He kept it there, spiked into Baldwin's back.

Ahead, the creek bent and the timber thinned.

Seeing the high, dark shapes of the picketed horses standing in the opening beyond the trees, Baldwin paused involuntarily. Stecker's first knocked him forward.

"Go on, *Lieutenant, sir,*" Ives crowed, no longer careful of his voice. "Call out if you want to. Won't help you now."

An awful apprehension was spreading over Baldwin. And an instinct faced him toward Stecker, who was paused strangely.

"He's your meat," Ives said, hurrying. "Get it over with."

Baldwin saw Stecker reseat his revolver and was puzzled for a moment. He saw Stecker's right hand go to a trouser pocket and come away and his two hands blur together. Baldwin heard a quick metallic snapping — it was the flick of a knife blade springing open in powerful hands. He took a backward step and felt the coil of pressure in his bowels and in his shallow breathing. He couldn't run. Both men stood near. Ives on his left, covering him with the carbine. Stecker three paces in front.

"Hurry up," Ives said, a peevish urging in his voice.

"I just want him to think about it a little while," Stecker ground out and his exultation rose. *"Think — Shoulder Straps — think!"*

Baldwin stood still, rigid. Then, as he spread his feet for Stecker's slashing rush, he felt a sudden protest. It was intolerable for a man to die like this. He pivoted low and fast and drove on bent legs, hurling his body to grope and whirl Ives between him and Stecker.

He heard the deafening roar of the carbine just before he ducked and struck Ives' body, and he got his hands on Ives and heaved him around. Horses were neighing and lunging on picket ropes. Another blast, which he took for Stecker's revolver, shattered while he fought Ives and wrestled for the carbine. It snapped free in Baldwin's hands, so suddenly he fell off balance.

For all his softness and lassitude, Ives had a terrier's quickness. He rushed in swiftly, clawing insanely for the short gun. In one motion, Baldwin sprang the Spencer's lever and eared back the hammer and fired.

Ives took the slug in his chest. It stopped him, it drove him back. He was falling when Baldwin, again working the carbine, flung around for Stecker.

But Stecker wasn't standing. He also was down and someone was running across the opening and calling, "Lieutenant — Lieutenant!"

Baldwin stood ready, not quite trusting the darkness. "Who is it?"

"Estep, sir. I shot one of 'em. I think it was Stecker."

Baldwin lowered the carbine, understanding about the second shot, and wondered if a man could be certain of anything on this violent, unpredictable night.

"Yes," he said. "That was Stecker you got."

Moonlight laid bare the faces on the ground. Stecker groaned and raised up a little, gagged and fell back. Ives didn't stir at all. The entire terrible finish had taken only moments, the space of a drawn breath.

Baldwin felt a vague sickness. He turned his gaze away.

"A white man . . . a trooper." Estep's voice dragged. "Makes you feel odd, sir."

"It does. Even after you know they intended to murder you."

"I heard! Just before you came by I thought I saw something moving around Ives' post. Ives never challenged, so I wasn't sure. But he did challenge you. . . . It didn't look right somehow. They were marchin' you off when I got over there." Apology was bitter in his voice. "They had you so close I couldn't risk a shot till now. . . ." Estep's voice dropped off on that faltering note.

"You did just right," Baldwin assured him.

Estep stood straight and still. He swayed — and lurched away, retching as he stumbled. Baldwin let him be, understanding; for he felt the same way.

New sounds penetrated. Troopers calling as they scouted through the dark woods. Somebody was on a horse. Baldwin went across the clearing and raised a shout and waited. Of a sudden he felt much older; he wondered maybe if the iron in him wasn't running out after all these years. His mind was searching and fumbling. Was tonight all of it? He hoped so fervently and knew he couldn't be certain. There was an incisive feeling that mined deeper than reason. Where was Van Horn?

Chapter 8

At sundown two days afterward Baldwin camped his command within sight of Fort Griffin, crouched on a hill overlooking the Clear Fork of the Brazos. He observed the looks of troopers in that direction and, therefore, had time to solidify his thinking on the matter when Sergeant Rooney asked for instructions.

"No one goes to the fort," Baldwin said, "except the men detailed with you to haul forage, commissary supplies and bring back the extra mules. I can't permit one man to drown himself in trader's rotgut when we're pulling out at daybreak. . . . Set out our usual pickets tonight. Tonkawas are generally camped along the river." He thought briefly of his new concern and continued. "Every day we're drawing closer to the settlements, and we all know how Texans regard Comanches. To be honest I'm more concerned about that little frontier village on the flat below the fort, it and the hide crews, than I am about warring Tonkawas or Comanches sneaking in after horses."

"What about Van Horn? He's been after me since we left Phantom Hill."

"If he goes, he won't be available for duty in the morning. He stays."

Rooney had no more than gathered his detail for the wagons when Baldwin spotted Van Horn coming. He crossed over briskly, in something of his former erectness. His blouse was buttoned and he had trimmed his moustache.

"I request permission to accompany the detail to the fort," he said, saluting, though unable to cover his intolerance of Baldwin.

"Request denied, Mr. Van Horn."

"I repeat the request."

"Nobody's going to hoorah the town, Van."

Van Horn fell into his flouting slouch. "Why wasn't I in that detail?"

"You want me to tell you why?"

"Hell, I know! Anything to remind a former fellow officer of his unjust demotion. I repeat —"

"Do so once more," Baldwin stopped him, "and you will hoof every inch of the way to Fort Belknap."

"Very well," Van Horn replied after a moment, adopting a pose of forced acceptance. "I haven't a chance in your command. I know that. However, you leave me curious about one thing." His inflamed eyes wore a sardonic amusement. "I notice Estep is going."

"Estep's no drinker. He's dependable."

"So I understand," Van Horn stated as only he could in his skirting, secretive air. "Very dependable."

"If you're trying to imply something, say it."

"I will — the truth!" Van Horn discarded all pretense. His jaw hung. His eyes gouged all their old resentment. He was breathing leakily through the hole of his querulous mouth. "You claim Stecker and Ives tried to murder you. . . . Wasn't it the other way around? You and Estep —"

Baldwin went hot. He started forward, then stopped. Holding his arms carefully down, he said, "Get out of my sight, Van. Immediately."

"Of course, Lieutenant. *Immediately.*" Van Horn flourished a hand over his heart and inclined his head, executing a burlesque bow. He snapped a precise salute, heeled about and set an exaggeratedly erect course for his wagon.

182

Watching the ridiculing figure, Baldwin perceived a clear-cut truth about himself. Once he had felt an acute sympathy for Van Horn; he had pitied him and wanted to help him. Now that was rubbed out. All of it.

It was after eight o'clock when he heard the rumbling of wagons bumping across the uneven approach to camp. The night wind carrying the rattles and creaks and jingles was still warm. He went out to watch them circle in. A horseman detached himself from the detail and Rooney said, "Big news at the fort. The colonel has just invaded Mexico. Took the whole regiment in and out. Came back with a passel of Kickapoo prisoners."

Baldwin let himself envision how the campaign must have been before he replied. Certainly it was galling to learn what they had missed, in exchange for their present thankless mission. "I shouldn't be surprised," he said. "That explains our single platoon. The colonel did need those men."

"Rest 'tis not so good," Rooney reported. "Been Indian raids northeast of us. Heavy between Belknap and Richardson. Officer of the Guard said he thought we'd be wise to lay over here a week."

"A week, a month — I can't see what we could gain. It can't be much rougher than what we've just had. No, we'll go ahead. I want to push on." The sergeant was reining away when Baldwin spoke again. "There's something I'd better square with you, Rooney."

"How's that, Lieutenant?"

"It's my fault you missed the campaign. I asked the colonel to transfer you from the second platoon."

"So that's how it came about? Now I'd best square up. See, while the lieutenant was down in San Antone a little bird whispered through the barrack one afternoon that a certain officer might take the heathens back north. So . . ." The sergeant seemed preoccupied.

"It takes you a long time to tell a story, Rooney."

"That it does when a man sees he's just small punkins after all. So I put in me request with the Captain McGregor. But all the time it was the colonel, not him, that said go an' here I was thinkin' I had drag with the captain! Good evenin', sor."

On the seventeenth day, during a driving rain storm, the train pulled across the last of a rolling plain and filed through the broken jaws of a stubby, wooded ridge guarding the west flank of the Salt Fork of the Brazos, opposite Fort Belknap. The intervening period seemed longer to Baldwin. He would have lost count of time had he not marked the days. It seemed that he could not remember when he wasn't pointing the pitching, canvas-backed wagons toward another obscure fort or risky crossing.

IIc rode down to the ford with Rooney and found the river booming. Where last autumn a placid stream had flowed, he saw a violent, copper-colored giant risen three times wide. He judged it while the cold filings of slanting rain struck his face and drummed against his rubber poncho. He eyed the little fort on the yonder side, its sandstone buildings looking ridiculously small and disconsolate through the misty light. Then he gave in and turned back up the grade.

He parked his wagons on a flat bench well above the river, using the ridge to his rear like an out-thrown picket line. Mitigating was the plentiful firewood supply of post oak and mesquite, and relief from Indian horse thieves while the rain fell. It continued throughout the first night and the second day. Mules and horses stood in heads-down misery. Troopers' tempers, already on edge, flared when shelter tents flooded and cooking fires hissed out. Smoke cloaked the bivouac at meal time, smarting eyes and throats. The Quahadas clung to their soaked canvas houses, suffering in silence. Baldwin ordered extra rations of bacon and coffee.

Thunderheads mottled the May sky on the third day, but did not loosen their flood. Presently the sun sneaked through and by nine o'clock the camp was steaming, bright and restless. Baldwin took a slippery ride to the drowned ford, hoping to see the river down. But the unpredictable Brazos was still roaring and brawling, high and wicked, full-voice.

Riding by the Pettijohn ambulance, he saw Rachel drying out sodden quilts.

"Good morning," she greeted him, and it stuck in his mind that not once on the trail had she displayed an early ill humor. "There's leftover coffee, still warm."

"Sounds good. I'm obliged to you."

He dismounted and she poured a cup and he said, "Looks like two days yet before we can cross. Means a lot of idle time. Just waiting." He sipped the strong coffee a while. The idea had come as he brooded on the way back from the river, and he presented it without preliminary. "A likely time — maybe — to start your school."

It was unexpected from him and left her astonished and elated. "The school? Why, yes, we could! While we wait! It would give the children something to do."

"Not an easy venture by any means," he cautioned. "You will have opposition from the older Indians. The witch woman, for one, will see sinister signs in the Bible. Your medicine book. It will be her medicine against yours. Superstition against . . . well, against the persistence of Quaker love."

She liked what he had said. He could see it in her face, and yet she seemed to appraise it for hidden irony and found none. "Thee surprises me with thy perceptions this morning," she said then, in open pleasure.

"Mostly old ones, based on what I've seen. Not heard or read about. It's best to know what you will face. You may be deeply disappointed."

"I've thought of that many times. What it would be like — what I would do that first day. It frightens me. In Pennsylvania, in college, I could see a pretty new schoolhouse with a shining bell that rang so clearly, and friendly Indian children passing inside as I stood at the door

187

smiling back at them." She looked away toward the river. "I know now it won't be like that. Facilities are primitive on the reservation at best. The children don't even know me and their parents detest a paleface woman. All of which I can well understand, Mr. Baldwin, in view of the violence they've experienced. That's why the truths of the Gospel will have to come later. After we've learned to trust each other." She was speaking rapidly, in eagerness. "So, first, I believe I should approach the children through play. Games — especially for the boys. Say, relay races. Doll-making for the girls. I have materials in the wagon."

Her excitement was beginning to affect him. "You will require the services of an interpreter. Rooney talks Comanche and sign. Might ask him."

"Sergeant Rooney. Of course!"

"All right, then. The games should take the romp out of these wild-horse Indian kids. Like drill for idling cavalrymen."

As he finished, the lively anticipation dimmed in her face and he saw the downward shift of her enthusiasm. "I wish thee hadn't said that."

"Why?"

"I'm not sure now. I don't know. Maybe I oughtn't try this. Not here. Without more preparation. Maybe the reservation is the proper place to start. Where surroundings are more peaceable. Conducive to teaching and learning."

To cover his surprise he set down his cup on a small camp table. "I don't understand. A moment ago you were in a rush to start." They faced each other in silence for several seconds. Something had spoiled the close feeling between them. He sensed that and he knew she did also. An insight kindled up, leaping to his mind. "You think I'm doing this just to keep the Indians occupied, don't you?"

Her reply was thought-out, searching. "I thought thee was doing it for them. So they might learn. Now I don't know. Everything keeps coming out horses, mules, wagons, rations — and *duty*. Not from the heart."

"Is it wrong to keep them out of mischief? Contented?"

"No. But is that all?"

Her reasoning nettled. He couldn't say; in truth he did not know. "When opposing people are thrown together as we are — like flint and dry powder — it's important they stay busy. Have specified duties. I can assure you of that. It cuts down unrest and grumbling. Never occurred to me I had to get pious and save heathen souls at the same time."

He saw the instant flick of feeling across her face. He saw hurt and wished he might recall the last. Before he could speak Corporal Higgins was tramping up from the lower picket lines, and Baldwin welcomed the diversion.

"Lieutenant," said Higgins, "I think my mount's got the heaves. Wonder if you'd take a look-see?"

"I'll be down in a minute."

Higgins tramped back and Baldwin looked at Rachel again. He had stung her. Her eyes showed it. Color laced her cheeks and she was breathing with composed anger, her breasts pressing high and rounded against her simple dress. Seeing her aroused and alive, he was softly stirred and reminded of the three-year gap in his living. And he knew it took stress to tear away the shell around her, to reveal the resolute young woman inside who, as yet, wasn't aware of being a woman.

"Sorry, Miss Pettijohn. My keen feelings got away."

"Thee thinks I expect too much of people?" she said, cool of voice.

"No doubt about it."

"But sometimes people reach beyond

themselves and make the world a little better."

"The world is an arena of sorts. Here, on the prairies or in the rowdy settlements. It's eye for an eye. Scalp for scalp. Kill or be killed. Root hog or die."

"No," she protested, trying to make him see. "Not *always*."

"You make yourself vulnerable when you try to change people. Shape them to your notions of what they ought to be."

"No — it's what they *can* be."

"Regardless," he pursued, unswayed, "it's risky business with Comanches."

"Like Topah and the medicine woman?"

"Just the medicine woman, maybe."

The determined line of her mouth relaxed. "Thee is contradicting thyself, Mr. Baldwin. Topah is superstitious, too."

"I happen to harbor a special dislike for that mesquite witch." He broke off on the realization that she had shifted the direction of their talk. "Well, that's all I have to say about the school. It's merely a suggestion. You do as you like. As you see it, the idea was worthy except for the spirit in which it was offered. Rather the lack of spirit. I can do no better. I'm a yellowleg cavalryman — no reformer. I've no sweetness and light to hoodwink Stone Age savages. My guess is, however, you'll find the Brazos no thornier than the reservation," he said and followed downhill after Higgins.

Higgins was right. His mount had a short, peculiar cough, symptomatic of the heaves, besides being a cantankerous halter-puller. Baldwin prescribed a copious concoction of saltpeter and rain water and spent a long while helping administer the remedy, finally pouring it down after running a forked stick through a strap fastened to the upper jaw, leaving the lower jaw free. He next started a detail cutting brush to fill the deep wagon ruts leading down to the ford. The morning was almost gone when he traveled back up the long slope, now drying fast underfoot in the hot sunlight.

He halted suddenly, as a surge of jubilant cries rushed across the brightness, and discovered the source where the short prairie grasses sparkled, bending in waves, and the bench flattened out. He had forgotten.

Indian children were racing back and forth in groups, girls as well as boys. Rachel stood at one side, Rooney the other. Between them everything was a swirl of movement. At this distance Rachel seemed scarcely taller than the oldest girls. Baldwin could hear Rooney's voice, dominant through the tumult of shrill Comanche. As Baldwin tarried, he was aware of a definite concord between the sergeant and the bird-like cries. Apparently it was Rooney's role to line up the racers, who then rushed toward Rachel. Elder Quahadas watching from the wagons were the lone sign of distrust. Or was it distrust? Baldwin wasn't sure.

He felt a powerful wish to go out there. Closer, so he might see the vivid expressions on the young faces. Such lively pleasures as this had been a rarity on the trail. It grew on him equally that he could not go. His presence would dampen the fun, perhaps end it. He admitted that with a mixture of regret, short of loneliness. He watched on and smiled to himself when he thought of Rachel's reluctance, watched until, finally, they tired and Rachel gestured to the wagons.

He left then, turning hurriedly out of sight behind a wagon so as not to be seen.

Neither did he intrude during the warm, still afternoon, when he saw Rachel and her audience of girls flocked around the ambulance. From what he could tell, she had spread out a bolt of calico, red with yellow flowers, and when not using scissors she appeared to be stuffing and folding and taking quick stitches with needle and thread. Out of these mystifying movements, as the day wore on, he started noticing children bearing quaint Quaker dolls. Always, it seemed, the older Indians hovered in the near distance like watching hawks.

Alone, Baldwin traveled north under a clear sky after breakfast the next morning, searching for an easier ford than the one below camp. The Brazos was lowering, though not fast enough to cross in clumsy wagons today. His purpose took him upstream for an hour or more; and finding no suitable place, he tracked back to come in behind the ridge fingers that curved with the bending river. Nowhere had he crossed Indian signs on the soft earth. But buffalo he did find not far from camp, scattered bunches of them grazing into the warm wind.

After tending and observing the train these days and nights, he had grown sensitive to its subtle variations of mood. The rise and fall of voices around the fires, a teamster's violent cursing, the sounds of the wagons in motion when all went well or badly, the settling quiet of evening, the restless stir of stock at night — these nuances told him something for better or worse.

Therefore, he noted the change soon after he entered the camp's north side. It was much too quiet; that came to him first. And the prairie where the children had romped yesterday was empty. Thinking they might be clustered around Rachel's wagon, he glanced there. He saw no one. The few Indians he found seemed carefully over by their wagons.

And Rooney seemed to be waiting for him. "School's out, Lieutenant. About an hour ago."

Baldwin measured him just a mild surprise, having learned long ago the unexpected was the train's trademark. "I take it you mean school is over for some time?"

"So it 'tis. Started off all right. We ran races a while. Then Rachel — I mean Miss Pettijohn — made some more dolls." Rooney permitted himself a rational shake of his head. "Man just can't tell about heathens. They watched every move we made. Eye-ball close. Pretty soon Miss Pettijohn got out her charts with animal pictures on 'em. She'd point to a horse or a buffalo or an eagle an' give the English word an' have the kids repeat it after her. Imagine her with buffalo pictures! That was something she knew Comanche kids would savvy sure enough."

"Then what started it?"

"The otter's picture — when she showed that. Glory! That old medicine woman climbed the sky! Threw a fit! Jumped up like she'd just rumped down on cactus. Claimed Rachel — I mean Miss Pettijohn — was stealin' her medicine power. Before I could explain or put up an argument — even be heard — the Indians rushed in, grabbed their kids an' back to the wagons they high-tailed it."

Baldwin nodded. "What does it take with these people, Rooney?"

"Time — a heap of time. Miss Pettijohn had the kids comin' her way, though. That she did."

"She try to stop the breakup?"

"No, sor. She just stood there. Like she expected it. She didn't lose her head. Didn't say a word. Just took it. She's whipped down now. Figures she's failed. Walked off down by the ford." Rooney raised a meaning look. "Me thought was the lieutenant, if he had a mind, could sorta talk to her —"

"Would the sergeant be meddling again?"

"Such would be me last act on this good earth," Rooney replied piously. "Only Miss Pettijohn's mighty discouraged, she is."

Baldwin was looking across camp at no specific object. He leaned thoughtfully back in the saddle and said, "I saw buffalo as I rode in. Northwest a few miles. Take some good shots. Try your luck."

"That I will! Fresh meat for supper." Rooney's blue eyes, beaming anticipation, sobered slightly. "Gettin' back to Miss Pettijohn —"

"Better assemble your outfit, Sergeant. Day's half gone."

Rooney beat evening's haze by a fair measure, filing in ahead of mules carrying meat bagged in the brown, furry hides. One string of mules he waved on to the troopers' tents; the other, which was longer, he halted. He called out in Comanche. A pause — and an Indian woman stood up and looked. She was old, but in that instant it was as if she had youth again. She whirled and shouted back and the shout was relayed down the wagons and instantly the Quahadas flowed from their resting places.

It wasn't long until the mingling smell of wood smoke and cooking buffalo meat and tallow pervaded the camp and made the mouth juices run. Mess fires leaped high and yellow. While the first meat cooked, women and children hurried for more mesquite and post oak. Long after the troopers had eaten, the Indians still gorged, and what wasn't consumed the women cut in thin strips and laid on racks for smoke-drying. There wasn't a harsh voice anywhere. A mantle of well-being covered the camp.

Baldwin savored the good scents, he listened to the comfortable sounds. He felt secure here, guarded by the swollen river and the wooded ridge. In all probability tonight would be the train's last bivouac free from all unease until it crossed Red River, a hard three days of traveling to the north.

Private Sullivan, taking his turn as orderly, materialized with the lieutenant's coffee, hard bread and buffalo supper on a tin plate.

"How's the arm?" Baldwin asked.

Sullivan couldn't mask his surprise. He mumbled. "All right, sir," and, with a look, walked away.

Baldwin ate his usual lonely meal and finished a cigar from his slender supply. His dim family connections were all but obliterated, save for an older brother in

Oregon whom he hadn't seen since the War and an aged aunt in Indiana. Time and great distances had further dulled his feeling of roots and home ties. He would be fortunate to die a captain, if that high, discouraging prospects at which he had railed as a younger man; now promotion seemed of less importance. He came to the image of himself and what he saw was not a satisfying one. He had followed too much the marble coldness of hard duty these past few years, seldom letting evident warmth creep in; when he did, as with Sullivan shortly ago, it was largely unsuspected and caused sudden embarrassment. Only Rooney knew him. And in driving himself as well as others he had left out the essential good times all men required on the frontier. He was, he felt, not unlike someone who had set a perverse course and, once embarked, knew not how to disengage from it.

He got up, in the grip of discontent and omission. Rooney knew. He should have talked to her. Moments afterward he walked out of the dark to Rachel Pettijohn's fire.

"Your prediction bore you out," he said, at once to the core. "My idea of the school here was premature, as you feared. You took the brunt of things today. I regret that."

"Thee's no cause to," she said, pleasant and undisturbed, when he had expected to find her otherwise. "The otter woman couldn't act any other way. I feel much better now."

"You make these days sound worthwhile."

"They have been. I know the children a little. They know me less. Anyway, they will be among those attending the agency school, and I shall count them among my first young friends."

"If their parents let them attend."

"They will — in time." She was young and yet she had an older knowledge. Her hands were busy clearing the small table as she spoke. She turned from him toward the white blooms of the Quahada wagons and the fire-lit figures moving there in the buckskin light. An old man was singing in a quavering voice: *Hi-yah, he-yah, hi-yah, he-yah*. There was a contentment in the old voice, Baldwin thought. A feeling for Indians and troopers. A piercing of the mystery that surrounded all people.

She said, turning back, "Thee was considerate to send the soldiers after buffalo. I know the captives are happier tonight than

I've ever seen them. I never heard them sing before."

"We needed fresh meat — that was all," he said, approaching curtness, and prepared to leave.

"Feasting helps them forget they are captives," she persisted, in a detaining voice. "Even the Jesus woman's school they distrust now."

"You're beginning to think like a Comanche." He was disapproving.

"If thee means I am wise, I am not. But I do know one truth," she said and he saw the long search of her eyes dwell on his face. "Even the unlovable change when they know they are loved. Oh, it doesn't take much — just a little. So very little, Mr. Baldwin. Giving them the buffalo meat has changed them tonight. Something has happened to them. Even you."

Disagreement was an audible harshness in his throat. "I was wrong. You don't know Comanches — *not yet*. Any Indian will fawn over you if it fills his belly. Then cut out your heart the next day." He went to the rim of the firelight. "At that they may need something extra in the next few days. Ourselves, too. Be traveling hard. We're near the settlements. Good night," he said and stepped out on his first tour of the guard posts.

Chapter 9

Overnight the copper-hued Brazos had fallen within its punished banks. Baldwin and Sullivan splashed abreast into the sluggish current, which swirled almost to their mounts' bellies. Sullivan employed an old notion of feeling out the sandy bottom by jabbing long sticks as he moved across. Some sticks stayed upright and some did not, but enough stood to mark the crossing.

Two rods from shore Baldwin saw the gouged-out strip of bank. At the same instant his gelding stepped off, floundered a moment and kicked out swimming. Sullivan's horse, on the right, went under simultaneously. Baldwin reined his mount left and humped up to higher footing, Sullivan following. They rode out upon the slanting bank, cut away for easier ascent.

"Swifter'n it looks," Sullivan swore, wet to his chest. "Have to mark that hole."

"Tell Rooney to warn every wagon."

Sullivan breasted back into the muddy water, jabbing, sticking. On the far slope wagons packed the rutted, brush-choked road down to the greasy ford.

Baldwin scanned the river once more. Sunlight lent it a placid look after the snarling flood. The crossing here had never been an easy one; its sands shifted and the current today possessed a deceptive swiftness.

He signaled come ahead.

The first three wagons took the stretch without accident, the mules swimming in places and finding footing again. They skirted the treachery of the deep hole ringed by Sullivan's punched-down sticks, and, agitated by the swirling pressure, flank muscles quivering, stormed up the slippery cut in walleyed rushes, flinging spray and sandy mud.

Rachel Pettijohn's ambulance came next. Estep had to stand up and whip his stubborn mules. They advanced obstinately, they edged down and struck the water, fought it a spell, and settled down to steady pulling. They were not midway across when the sticks marking the hole keeled over, swept away.

Baldwin called in warning, "Swing higher up."

He saw Rachel, on Estep's right, look up suddenly. He saw Estep nod and yank and slant up stream, saw him holding an angling course and the mules bending to the pull of the current. Baldwin couldn't tell just where the jump-off was now, and knew that Estep, in struggle, could tell less. Baldwin shouted again. Estep hauled harder around and the mules kept yawing stubbornly, eager, instead, to bear straight across.

Estep's face knotted in greater strain; gradually, sawing on the reins, he strong-armed the mules about a notch. No more. Not enough, Baldwin feared, gauging the hole's approximate location.

His shout was late; it happened too fast. He saw everything at once — Estep's right lead mule plunging down, only its head showing, terrified, eyes wild, and the right front wheel of the ambulance dropping as suddenly and Rachel falling out, thrown clear, the greedy current sweeping her under.

Baldwin heard men hollering, words that lost distinctness as he crow-hopped his balky horse off the bank and hit the water. This wasn't the lazy Brazos of mid-summer. It was hell-bent and treacherous here in the deepest part of the channel, wrenching and tearing at a man's legs and arms.

His eyes missed her. Fear raked him. He urged the horse down river — and saw a blur of white. Reaching out, he grabbed and caught hold of cloth and felt an arm. He pulled her closer. She wasn't struggling at all. She was limp and her head rolled, an inertness that stirred him faster. He managed an arm under her shoulders and, lifting her against the saddle, struck out for shore. Above them the ambulance was skittered around, tail end to the river's run. Sullivan was out there, one hand fisted on a mule's bridle as he guided the teams toward the cut.

In front of Baldwin appeared the eroded section of reddish bank. Above, he could see men stiff and watching. The gelding's forequarters rose, its hoofs churned. The bank crumbled, the horse fell back and sank deeper and Baldwin, seeing the ambulance blocking the ford, reined with the current, swimming the animal.

They came out rods below, where the bank straightened. Mueller ran over and drew Rachel down, stretched her out as Baldwin dismounted and bent over her.

Her continued inaction worried him. She was breathing, but looked terribly pale. Then, in understanding, he saw the small, bluish lump on her forehead. She looked slim and so very young, with the sodden clothing pressing the folds of her small-boned body. Her yellow hair, still knotted severely, accented her pallid face. He rubbed her wrists.

"She's coming to," Mueller said, relieved.

She opened her eyes; they were big and round and questioning. She became slowly aware of the faces over her.

"You were knocked out," Baldwin said, leaning back. "Must have bumped your head on a wagon brace when you pitched out." Other troopers were hurrying over. He turned to them, his command curt. "Get a blanket."

Rachel sat up and Mueller snugged his blouse around her. She pressed a hand to her forehead. "All I remember was falling into the water. Being unable to move. Though it wouldn't have made much difference. I can't swim. How did I get here?" She looked around for someone to complete the story.

"Why, ma'am, the lieutenant dragged you out," Mueller said.

Baldwin, seeing what was coming by Mueller's face, was turning before Mueller finished, going off to the dripping ambulance and its bedraggled mules drawn up away from the ford.

"Everything all right?" he asked Sullivan, and discovered that he was thinking of Miss Pettijohn's school supplies.

"Just a little wet, looks like. Ambulance never did go over."

Baldwin centered his attention across the river. More wagons waited and the sun was climbing. He spoke an order to Sullivan. "Have Rooney place men on each side of the mules to assist if necessary. Tell him to swing extra wide next time. We're losing time."

Mueller was assisting Rachel to her wagon. Seeing Baldwin, she came up to him and paused. Color had returned to her cheeks. She hugged an issue blanket around her.

"There wasn't time to thank thee," she said.

"Not necessary. Fortunately, I ride a stout horse. Better get into dry clothes." His speech cut across hers. He was abrupt without meaning to be, and dismissing. He ruled out further talk by passing on to get his horse.

He was riding back to the ford when he heard her clear voice inquiring about the school supplies, and it occurred to him that another woman would have asked first about her personal belongings. Well, there was a bottle of brandy in his wagon. She should have that whether she approved or not. He would have Mueller take it over to her.

Riding up the slope to Fort Belknap, Baldwin saw nothing cheering to the eye. An angry conviction stood out: at a time when Indian troubles had never been heavier, all the posts between Fort Sill and Concho were steadily going to hell, year by year, piece by piece, stone by stone, never mended or kept up, prime examples of government neglect.

Belknap, alone in a wilderness of sandstone and mesquite, was even smaller than Fort Chadbourne and just as tumbledown. Like Chadbourne, it had spent its youth recklessly before the War and subsequent oversight had speeded its ruin. Seeing the broken stone commissary and two barracks, the old headquarters and grain storage and powder magazine, he had the marked regret for a post deliberately forgotten years ago and yet expected to protect a vast region. Belknap was so poor it had neither stables nor stockade and was forced to picket its mounts.

A forlorn-looking first sergeant on a lean horse met him beside the rutted road curling up from the bottomland. Not only did the man salute, he shook hands warmly. Loneliness hung in his eyes, plus a ground-in wariness.

"Been watching you through the glasses, sir. Big outfit."

Baldwin was thinking ahead. "What's the situation east of here?"

"Hell. Been plain hell all spring. Since pony grass turned green." The sergeant's knowing eyes hooked on the coming-up wagons. "Sure don't envy you with that bunch of Indians, Lieutenant. You have to go to Fort Richardson?"

"Destination is Fort Sill."

The man's harried expression increased. He pursed his mouth and was hesitant.

"Speak up, Sergeant."

"You better know this now, sir. Feeling is running high in Jacksboro. Everybody's stirred up. Been raids all around. Comanche an' Kiowa. Killing and stealing. A cowboy was wounded and scalped alive last week within sight of town. Three travelers had their horses stolen. A few days back seven freighters with Collins and Weybright got ambushed west of Cox Mountain on Salt Creek Prairie. One —

they say — was found chained to the wagon tongue over a fire with his face to the ground. And that's the way it's been, Lieutenant."

"I see — the usual. And just what are they doing about it at Fort Richardson? Or able to do?"

"Chasing heat devils, sounds like. Not enough to suit the citizens you can bet." His lonesomeness built back; it filled his eyes and thinned his mouth. "We don't see much here. Don't hear much. I hate to see you head that way with Indians, Lieutenant. 'Pears to me you got to watch out for both sides. Unless you move fast. Night march, maybe. Sneak past Jacksboro into the fort."

"In which event I'd still have to come out again soon," Baldwin said, scowling over the information, worse even than he had expected. He looked to the rear and saw that all wagons had cleared the river flat, and turned again to the sergeant, considering, remembering his own lonely duty in similar posts, and ventured a guess.

"How many in your garrison? Ten, fifteen?"

"Eight, sir."

"How long since you've had any tobacco?"

"About a month. Lucky to get our mail now an' then."

"Well. See that fellow back there on the gray horse? The one bawling out the trooper on the wagon? Needless to say, that is Sergeant Rooney. Ride back and tell him I said to issue you two weeks' tobacco rations."

Baldwin placed his wagons two abreast instead of single file, ordered flankers and advance riders out and trotted smartly eastward on the stage road to Jacksboro and Fort Richardson. Into the afternoon they moved in that vigilant readiness across rolling prairie, alert to circle left and right into a quick corral. Bluish haze coated the distant ridges. Baldwin could see for miles, and the air was dry.

At four thirty he sighted the north branch of Flint Creek, which edged a broad plain of scattered mesquite sloping on toward Cox Mountain. Sensitive, cat-footing country: Salt Creek Prairie. An innocent-sounding name for such criss-crossed, bloody ground, this passageway for Indian bands coming and leaving. Plain to the eye, just off the road in a broken circle, lay the burned hulks of the teamsters' wagons. To the north sat a conical sandstone hill and along its foot sprang thin ranks of scrub oak lining the branch. Indians taking position on the hill thus commanded the three open miles to the mountain. Last year Baldwin's command had counted twenty-one crude head boards scattered up and down the road over the shallow graves of teamsters, cowboys and stage travelers buried where they had fallen.

Baldwin bunched his wagons along the thinly wooded branch for night bivouac.

"I prefer this position for two reasons," he told Rooney.

"We can see around us and we've the sandstone lookout at our rear. Post pickets there tonight. On east I don't like at all. We're too close to the settlements."

Sundown fell in streamers of scarlet and the long day, retreating, shed the mealy gray of dusk for the deep purple of late evening. Orange-yellow fires traced the camp's close-in shape. Outside, Rooney grazed the mules and horses under guard for an hour and drove them inside.

After dark, Baldwin heard a horse trotting west on the stage road. A sentry's challenge braced the traveler. Voices mixed and a white man, leading his mount, entered the light of the troopers' main cooking fire. He stopped when halted by the confronting presence of Baldwin.

"Saw your fires," the man said. "Don't mind sayin' I smelled supper, too."

Baldwin sized him up. He was gangly and hatchet-faced, of roving eye and mouthing a drollness. By his nondescript appearance he could be a town hanger-on, ranch hand or out-law or anybody. He gave off a purposeful vagueness and designed anonymity, countered by the walk-in boldness that Baldwin felt was intrusive.

"You're welcome to supper," Baldwin said. "Tie up to that wagon."

The man nodded. Leaving his horse, he returned to the fire, *phutted!* out an egg-size wad of tobacco and took a tin plate and coffee cup. Instantly he was wolfing bacon and hard bread in enormous, noisy gulps.

Baldwin said, "Aren't you taking chances, riding alone across Salt Creek Prairie?"

"Not the first time. I'm used to it. Out lookin' for horses the Injuns took."

"You live in Jacksboro?"

"Thereabouts."

"We've noticed no horses or Indians."

"Nobody can hide horseflesh like a god-damned greasy, sneakin', stinkin' Indian."

"Indians," Baldwin said, projecting his thoughtful cynicism. "It's always Indians."

"Got a better notion?"

"Many times it is Indians, I agree. But it seems a little strange to me, the frontier stand that no one but an Indian has reason to steal horses." He didn't know why he was differing and defending, unless it was the increasing irritation the man aroused in him.

The visitor squatted forward. "How y'figure that?"

"Early this spring," Baldwin said, "troops at Fort Richardson chased what they thought were Indians who had stolen post mounts. Gunfire was exchanged. One of the thieves fell. His friends rode on. Got away. At first glance the dead man looked like an Indian. Closer inspection showed he was white, disguised as an Indian. False hair, mask, buckskin leggings and so forth."

"Never heard it."

"It happened."

Soaking hard bread in his coffee, the white man finished both and scrubbed the back of one dirty hand across his bearded mouth. He fished his glance across the bivouac, back and forth over the Quahada wagons. "How far you come today?"

"Fort Belknap." Baldwin's nod was bare.

"Comanch' or Kioways you got along?"

"Comanches."

"About how many?"

"About what you see." Which, from Baldwin's estimate, was about one-third their number.

The white man looked down the long blade of his nose. "Rather drive hogs, myself."

A sudden quiet pushed down. Rooney stiffened. He was staring hard when Baldwin, ignoring the remark, said, "If you were in the army, you would escort Indians whether you took a shine to it or not."

"Except I ain't in the army," came the amused reply. "Yes, sir, you boys got a stinkin' chore. Be in Jacksboro and Fort Richardson tomorrow, though."

"Those are my plans," Baldwin said, unmistakable, and saw Rooney's eyes pin him, glaring censure. "Our stock is worn down," Baldwin went on. "Probably be late afternoon before we pass through town."

The sparse talk fell away. After helping himself to a third cup of coffee, the white man stood and wiped greasy palms on the thighs of his britches. One corner of his mouth curled, scattering the provoking drollness. He said, "Tell Uncle Sam I'm much obliged for the vittles," and untied his horse. He was out of sight in moments, drumming hard.

"I know what you're thinking," Baldwin said to Rooney. "He rode in from the east and he's riding back east now. One man hunting horses on Salt Creek Prairie at night. I don't believe him either."

"Sure — an' why did the lieutenant have to give our line o' march, too? Tell me." Rooney spoke from the stiff height of an old soldier's prerogative. "Into Jacksboro — on to the fort, ye said. Arrive late in the afternoon, we will. Oh, the lieutenant laid it out in detail. So very helpful-like. By domn, I didn't care for the likes o' that fine cutthroat. Too nosey. Gobbled our grub, insulted us, gave up the eyeball inspection an' pranced off."

"Agreed," Baldwin said.

Rooney cocked a suspicious eye. "Would the lieutenant be holdin' out on us, now?"

"Hardly that," Baldwin said and laid his wry smile on the sergeant. "Just waiting for that Irish temper of yours to come down from boil." His voice slipped lower, grave. "Let that white man think we're going into Jacksboro. Let him — because we're not. We're going around the town and then some. Cutting across country to Red River. I've been considering it all day."

Rooney's stare widened. "Means we miss Richardson."

"Have to — with Jacksboro between us."

"That it is."

"Several things are in our favor," Baldwin said, displaying to them a confidence he wished he felt. "By skirting the settlements we're also avoiding trouble. It's open country to the Red. By tomorrow night we should be out of reach. Our wagons are in stout condition. Most of our mules are serviceable, thanks to the rest on the Brazos. . . . We will form our train as we did today, two wagons abreast. Corporal Higgins will hold the rear guard within seventy-five to one-hundred yards tomorrow. Same for the flankers. The advance, under Corporal Pierce, will maintain a distance not exceeding two hundred yards. Stay within easy sight of the train."

He trailed his eyes over the circle of earnest faces, becoming aware of how openly he was speaking to these men. It was the first time. In the past he would have called Rooney aside and instructed him alone, or, as he had above Mountain Pass, assembled the noncoms, which also had been uncommon for him. Tonight he was just talking, and plainly. Seeing their nods, he knew he had said enough.

"Feed extra grain," he said, a trace of curtness in his voice. "Break camp at four o'clock."

He walked the outposts and was returning to the wagons when Van Horn crossed in front of him and spoke.

"May I present my compliments?"

"I know of no compliment you'd have for me."

"I was referring to your remarks at mess," Van Horn said and bobbed his head in the slightest of mocking bows. "A most touching address, my general. Designed, no doubt, to bring forth the highest sense of duty in the underpaid minions who serve a thankless army."

"A shame you can't do as well — you, a former officer," Baldwin replied, trying not to rise to the bait of pointless argument.

"If leadership were of any concern to blind martinets like Mackenzie, you and I would find ourselves bearing the exact opposite ranks we do tonight." He dropped one slurring shoulder, and although it was too dark to see Van Horn's face clearly, Baldwin could picture his expression of intolerance. "But back to your address. Is the weight of command so burdensome you have to share it with these ignorant clodhopping bumpkins you call troopers?"

Something tore loose in Baldwin. He was moving swiftly. He found his hands tearing at Van Horn's blouse, and he was shaking Van Horn and muttering, "Why, goddamn you — you're not enough to lick the boot soles of any one of 'em!" He threw Van Horn to the ground and stood over him, breathing in soggy gulps. He started to pick Van Horn up, but straightened and said, "This is your last duty with me. Now get the hell back where you belong."

Van Horn found his feet. His face was blurred. He pulled once on his blouse and for a long-held breath Baldwin could feel the bitter ill will pouring out of the man as if released through a broken dam. It was more than intolerance or jealousy now; it was a synthesis of everything gone wrong in Van Horn. It was towering and blaming and blind, and therefore dangerous, and more appalling and terrible than Stecker's hate, which had been uncomplicated, generated by the single desire to destroy.

"You laid hands on me,' Van Horn said. "You shouldn't have touched me at all."

He slouched away and Baldwin walked on to his quarters, always at odds with himself after Van Horn had shaken his self-control.

He fell asleep almost at once, but his rest was uneasy. A dream of futility filled his mind. He was struggling in the coppery waters of the Brazos. Van Horn stood on the slick, steep bank. Whenever Baldwin struggled to climb out, Van Horn kicked him back. Again and again Baldwin reached the shore, and each time Van Horn, wearing a major's leaves, mocked him with obscenities and thrust a boot against his bleeding face.

. . . Rooney's voice outside the ambulance jumped Baldwin awake.

"What is it?" Baldwin answered.

"It's Van Horn. He went over the hill — sneaked his horse off the picket line."

"What's the hour?"

"Three o'clock."

Chapter 10

Baldwin sent the train stringing out by first light, eastward along the pale tracings of the stage road for half a mile, past the broken skeletons of the teamsters' wagons, ghostly in the gray-black murk, and then north in double file, away from Cox Mountain.

Dawn, full strength, laid the land open to the encompassing blue eye of the clean sky. On all sides the bright country flowed away in rippling undulations of short, curly buffalo and grama grasses, far, far, until the gaze blurred. It was also empty as a hat. Baldwin could remember great masses of buffalo ranging between the Brazos and the Little Wichita River and on to the Red. But last autumn hide crews had begun slipping out of Kansas, violating the ban against buffalo hunting south of the Arkansas. Some, obviously, had worked down here and moved on, as evidenced by patches of bleached bones. A slaughter calculated to ruffle Comanche tempers still more.

They halted at ten o'clock to rest the mules and made onward again. Afterward, they nooned on the open prairie.

"What do you make of Van Horn?" Baldwin asked Rooney.

"It's been comin' a long time."

"We had a little scuffle last night. That set him off. Still, I'm surprised. He knows what it means to desert. Once done there's no turning back."

"I think I know why," Rooney said, looking grim. "He's from the same tribe as Ives an' Stecker. Just works in a different fashion. Those two thought with their hands most times, though Ives could use his head. They used guns or knives. Van Horn — he's the other kind, but just as mean. Just as dangerous; maybe worse. Thinks he's the only man God ever gave a speck of brains to. The only man in the army fit to be an officer. He thinks cute. Maybe he went over the hill, Lieutenant, just to spite you. Ever think of that?"

Rooney had never seen the inside of a schoolhouse past the sixth grade, but his judgment concerning men, gleaned from barrooms, drill fields, the War and Indian skirmishes, was generally close to the mark.

Baldwin shook his head in a wondering way. By common assent, they dropped the matter.

That night they camped on a creek which flowed northeast into the Little Wichita River. Baldwin felt an increasing confidence. No settlements lay between the train and Red River; encountering wrathy Texans so far north was unlikely now. Just Indians possibly. Indian stock thieves or a war party heading for the battered settlements around Jacksboro.

He saw the same emptiness on the second morning as they crossed the Little Wichita and struck a straighter course north.

The hot afternoon wore away, the hours passing in monotonous, single file, the train dipping and rising over the heaving prairie ocean; other times, when the footing roughed, it was as if imprisoned caterpillars were squirming and wriggling inside each string of oscillating canvas tops. And subtly the land was changing, sloping toward the Red in massive sweepings.

Daylight was weakening when Baldwin raised his glasses and picked up a low, brown, uneven line far to the north, vague through the haze of distance. What he saw was the north side of the Red, the higher side, where the bluffs made a broken stand. Seeing it acted as a spur. After fording the narrow Wichita River at dusk, he pressed ahead and changed course to the west, aiming for the ford that let travelers across into Indian Territory and led on to Fort Sill. His firm intention was to camp late that night on the banks of the Red and cross in the morning.

A mile past the Wichita, Corporal Higgins galloped up from the rear. His worried eyes spoke before he said, "Better come back for a look, sir. Big bunch of riders right on us."

Baldwin resisted the impulse to go immediately. He told himself it couldn't happen after the unbroken two days and the distance traveled without hindrance. His hesitation was brief, in the lapse it took for his illogical unwillingness to admit the gravity he saw in the sun-flamed face. He rode back to the rear guard, which was following slowly in the train's wake, and halted, looking off south.

To the naked eye the horsemen seemed a dark, low cloud skimming across the darkening green swells of prairie. White men.

Hunters? No, he decided. There were too many. And not without wagons.

He uncased his glasses and raised them, dreading to look. He pressed tighter against his eyes, adjusting. He saw riders in a loose wedge. A strong two hundred or more; the number sat in him with shock. Every man seemed to carry a rifle or shotgun.

Baldwin was conscious of a black certainty. He cased the glasses and turned to Higgins. "Tell Rooney to corral at once. Keep all the Indians under cover. He is not to fire unless we are fired on out here. Tell him to shoot any white man who tries to force his way inside the circle."

Higgins rushed away and Baldwin motioned the three-man rear guard to fall back. When the wagons had swung out, left and right, forming quickly, he halted the detail and said, "Draw carbines. Just hold them across your saddles." As for himself, he unloosened the flap on his holster, but left the revolver there.

He could hear them coming a long way off, yipping and calling. Some of them reeling. He could see them standing in stirrups and brandishing weapons. There was no semblance of order. It was a frontier crowd, a mob; to make matters worse, a drunken mob. Here and there riders waved bottles.

Baldwin glanced behind him. Rooney had the wagons circled neatly, the teams turned inward.

Baldwin leaned forward as the noisy horsemen slanted down a long rise and the discord fell stronger, the steady drumming of so many horses the prairie was trembling.

At about twenty-five rods he raised his right hand in a stopping motion. These men, riding with reckless ease, did not slow at all.

He stiffened — were they going to overrun him? — and willed himself to stand his ground.

They drew on another five, eight, ten rods and checked up, the loose folds of the jostling riders lapping over at the ends, forming an irregular crescent.

Baldwin sized them up and his previous estimate of their number didn't change. Cowmen and townsmen, he saw, plus a wild mixture of frontier rowdies along for the fun.

Two men rode out from the center. Their horses were packed with blankets and camp gear for a long ride. Baldwin looked and felt a stab of surprise as he recognized the hatchet-faced "horse hunter" of Salt Creek Prairie.

"That's him," the man said and pointed at Baldwin.

It was the other who took up from there, an erect, middle-aged rider whose left sleeve was empty, pinned prominently to his shoulder, Baldwin thought, like a badge of honor.

"I am Quincy — Solomon Quincy," he boomed out, "and I will state our business short and sweet, sir."

"I am Lieutenant Baldwin. Fourth Cavalry."

Quincy wasn't drunk, but the tone of his speaking was undeniably pompous, such as when he dwelled extra long over giving his name, and he held his head turkey-cock high. Vain, opinionated, blustery, Baldwin put him down, but no fool. Solid and hard to move once set. Brows as bushy as a bird's nest and a large nose and heavy though precise lips mostly lost behind the impressive black thicket of moustache and beard.

"Lieutenant," he said, "we know there are Comanche bucks in your train. We want them. We are goin' to hang them. Every last murderin', gut-eatin' heathen."

"By whose authority?"

"By authority of the long-suffering citizens of the state of Texas, sir! We are vigilantes — organized in defense of our homes and ranches. Doing what your army can't do or refuses to do."

"We are trying, Mr. Quincy. You should know how tough it is."

"I know we've had raids all spring. Seven teamsters murdered on Salt Creek Prairie just four days ago. My own son killed by Comanches in the Nations six weeks ago while taking cattle up the trail."

"I am sorry," Baldwin said earnestly and selected his next words with extreme care. "And I'm glad to point out that the Indians in this train didn't commit the recent attacks you just named. They've been government prisoners at Fort Concho since their capture last fall on McClellan Creek."

"They're Comanches — heathens."

"You would hold them responsible for acts they didn't do?" Baldwin replied and realized that he had raked up one of Rachel Pettijohn's arguments, one she had used against him.

"What does that prove, where they were captured? They've all stolen Texas stock and killed our people, one time or another. Hell, man, a Comanche's a Comanche — a wild varmint, sir — to be shot on sight. Exterminated. I say kill the seed and there will be no fruit."

"My orders are to deliver these Indians to Fort Sill. The government feels their return will serve to keep more Comanche bands peaceful and out of Texas." Baldwin dared not mention Hard Shirt, for fear that notorious raider's presence would whet the Texans' demands.

"The day Comanches quit raiding in Texas there will be a blizzard in hell," Quincy tossed back. "My fast-talking Yankee friend, you are outnumbered ten to one. Let's be reasonable and avoid any unnecessary effusion of blood. Hand over those bucks."

"I have no intention of disobeying my orders. Besides not being so defenseless as you say, I should inform you that two companies of cavalry were scheduled to depart Fort Richardson this afternoon for Fort Sill."

Quincy and the other man exchanged looks of hard amusement. "Two companies?" Quincy went on, appearing to speak from a superior knowledge. "Now I will tell you something. You did surprise us when you slipped off north, instead of traveling on through Jacksboro; and you were wise not to venture there, the way folks are worked up." His tone changed, brushing an admiration he was loath to reveal. "You've moved your train more than sixty miles in two days. You almost got away. But it happens we know everything about your train, Lieutenant. Your route. The strength of your escort down to the last man. The exact number of Indians. And there are no two companies. You've had no communication with the fort. You're just bluffing. You're all the blue-bellies there are between Fort Richardson and Red River."

Baldwin did not contradict. His mind was groping sickly, feeling, fastening. He said, "Your remarks about United States cavalry prompt me to remind you the War's over."

"*That* one might be," Quincy said, expelling an old bitterness, and tapped his empty sleeve. "This one's not. Our craws are full, sir. We are in the right. One of the psalms says, 'Thou shalt bruise them with a rod of iron, and break them in pieces like a potter's vessel.' "

"I cannot recall any mention of Comanches in the Old Testament, Mr. Quincy."

"It refers to *enemies* — and Comanches are that, God knows," Quincy said, his eyes burning.

Turned restless by the palavering, the horsemen were milling, creating a noisy undertone, and the sharp-featured man beside Quincy seemed to voice their feeling. "We're not celebratin' the Fourth of July, Quincy. Cut out the speeches. Let's get down to taw."

"Kelso," Quincy said and turned in the saddle, "you men voted me in as your captain because of my long service during the War. In turn, I remind you that I will conduct surrender negotiations in the proper manner or not at all. If any of you do not wish to serve under my command, you may turn tail for Jacksboro."

"Just get on with it," a man called.

"I intend to," Quincy shut him off, "but it will be done properly." He faced Baldwin again. "Lieutenant, it's talk on the barrelhead now. You have one buck we want above all. It's that Hard Shirt, who has raided through here many times."

"All the bucks are old men," Baldwin said, fighting his surprise. "Not a warrior among them."

"Would you question the word of one of your own troopers?" Quincy said, hurling Baldwin his triumph. He motioned behind him. "Show him, boys."

An opening was made in the press of

horsemen, leaving a single rider there.

Baldwin didn't recognize him the first instant, for it was a different Van Horn. Sight of him might have stirred Baldwin's dim pity in other days; now he could feel only a sickened and deeply driven anger as all things became clear.

Van Horn had rid himself of all soldierly accouterments, complete to high-horned stock saddle and another horse. He wore new pantaloons and boots, a checkered vest and wide-brimmed hat. His vest hung open, his coat was tied across the saddle. He tipped a bottle toward Baldwin and with the other hand removed his hat in a sweeping bow of formal mockery.

Quincy's voice scattered a cold cheerlessness. "One of the vicissitudes of war, my friend."

"He'll stand court martial yet," Baldwin swore.

"Do we get the bucks without bloodshed?"

"I won't surrender them."

"Then we will take them."

"I warn you there are Indian women and children back there."

"We have seen what happened to settlers' families, sir."

"There's also a young white woman — a

Quaker missionary going to the reservation."

"We know about her. They're all your responsibility."

"I'm not certain I could persuade them to leave the train."

"In that event, sir, your decision is made for you. You can give up with honor."

"Just how is that?" Baldwin asked cynically.

"Release the bucks to prevent possible injury to the white woman and Indian families. Your superiors would agree under such circumstances. The lives of a great many in exchange for a handful of greasy Comanches."

"No," said Baldwin, feeling the quick strike of his disgust, and suddenly he had established what was left him. *Delay, delay.* Be firm and still call upon every possible approach to reason; for one heedless, angry retort by himself might hurl them against the thinly protected wagons. He had found reason to suspect a division within the mob's leadership. But although Quincy and Kelso might differ as to the means, they agree on the end; that was clear.

Quincy's eyes squeezed in and he puckered his mouth, underlip rolled out. "I will make you another proposition. Release Hard Shirt and we will let the others go with you. But Hard Shirt we must have."

"I can't do that."

Quincy's sigh was dry as dust. "You leave us no alternative."

"There is one. You're a soldier, Mr. Quincy. I request your indulgence for more time."

Kelso stuck his long face in, jowls shaking. "By God, we won't be put off."

"All I'm asking is a truce until tomorrow morning," Baldwin said. "We can't get away, we can't get word out."

"I won't agree," Kelso said.

"We're corralled for a fight. My men are all veterans. We fought our way through Mountain Pass. We won't be buffaloed by a drunken mob."

"You blue-bellies will see how drunk we are in a fight."

Quincy said, "What purpose would a truce serve? You've already decided not to give up the bucks."

"Can I persuade the Indians — from here — to get their families out of the way? Can I the young white woman?"

"I'm against any truce," Kelso complained.

Baldwin's derision was for Quincy alone.

"I trust you're not making war on women and children?"

"We can take the wagons right now," Kelso urged.

"You can try," Baldwin said, still watching Quincy. "Just keep in mind we're armed with Spencer repeaters — effective up to five hundred yards. Something Mr. Quincy no doubt can recall from his war experiences." Baldwin was knotted with the bleak comprehension of having exhausted all arguments. He was gambling on Quincy, who as yet gave no sign.

Seizing on Quincy's silence, Kelso turned scornful. "Aim to let a little peawaddin' bunch of Yankees bluff you out?"

That, Baldwin sensed, was the poorest approach Kelso should have tried.

"I am in command," Quincy said and flashed Kelso his offense. Spots of red appeared under his eyes as Quincy turned back, and Baldwin knew not what to expect, either way. "You say you want time to talk to the white woman and the Indians?"

"Yes," Baldwin said and saw what was bothering Quincy: it was the white woman most of all. "Furthermore, I can't see palavering until your men sober up in the morning."

"You will make efforts to separate the

noncombatants from the bucks?"

"I will. I also request permission for my watering details to pass through your lines back to the river."

"Fair enough. I am a gentleman and a soldier, sir. If you are successful in separating your people, I will guarantee safe conduct through my command. There is one other condition to the truce. . . . Be prepared to surrender the bucks — all of them, mind you — at sharp daybreak. Otherwise, we attack. I mean that. We attack even if the women and children and the young missionary worker are still inside your circle. Their safety rests with you. I hope Yankee cavalry hasn't taken to hiding behind a woman's skirts."

"You would attack United States troops?" Baldwin asked, finding one final argument.

"Sir," said Quincy. His voice was like a spike, his eyes glowing with a determined light. "I assure you that never stopped me in the past. Do we understand each other?"

"I'm afraid I do."

Grumbling broke out after Quincy finished. Kelso stared his glittery dissent, but no man questioned Quincy's command.

Riding back through growing twilight, Baldwin grasped certain conclusions. Humaneness had not entirely prompted

Quincy's agreement to the truce. Some of his men were too drunk to fight effectively. His horses looked tired, the hour was late, and the corralled wagons promised stiff resistance. Beyond these observations, however, Baldwin didn't delude himself. The respite was temporary. He had contrived only to delay. In Quincy he recognized a man cocked to fight, brooding over the loss of his son, self-righteous, bullheaded, moved by public opinion and his own narrow code. He would attack if necessary to get the bucks, reconciling in some occult way that he and Providence rode under the same banner.

Baldwin's mind caught. He was staggered by what else he saw with frightening clarity — a part of himself, a reflection, a reminder of his own inflexible hardness in Solomon Quincy. *It was morally right to kill Comanches*. If innocents happened in the way and suffered, that was unfortunate but right had been done. *Bruise them with a rod of iron*.

A drum of sound reached him. He saw Quincy leading the main body of horsemen around to take positions on the north side, blocking off the train from the Red. Other riders were scattering out to complete the encirclement.

Chapter 11

Baldwin rode inside the corral, followed by the rear-guard, and dismounted, sensing that all eyes watched him. Some portent must have shown on his face, because when Rooney came across, he fell silent after one glance and waited for Baldwin to speak. Baldwin told him concisely, omitting nothing.

"Van Horn!" Rooney swore grimly. "Ah, how I'd like to get me hands on that fine gentleman."

"He'll be picked up if he hangs around Jacksboro," Baldwin predicted. "If not, his own particular hell will take care of him in time."

" 'Tis not soon enough for me. . . . So we've got till daybreak?"

"Unless the drunks cause trouble earlier. Set out pickets beyond the wagons, then let's have one hell of a big supper before we palaver with the Indians."

Rooney shook his head doubtfully and began calling out troopers' names as a man might bite off chunks of iron.

Night was a low-flying hawk swooping down all at once, its dark wings brushing the wagon tops, its arrival both welcome and dreaded. His pickets could detect any sudden rush and give warning; meanwhile, surrounded, encumbered with wagons, he couldn't slip away. As the wind fell and the train became quieter, noises jarred from Quincy's encampment not four hundred yards away. Now and then a gun banged; whoops lifted.

Only the children stirred much in the train. Not, it ran through his mind, because they failed to understand the threat of guns and white men — they did, being Comanche children and survivors of McClellan Creek. But, thankfully, they were too young to know a lasting fear. A game or a simple cedar doll or one of Rachel's quaint Quaker dolls commanded more immediate attention tonight. He watched them, affected sharply by his own hard responsibility and the lack of any real alternative. He thought, *Let them play.*

He waited until all supper sounds dissolved, and he sensed the Quahadas also waited. Standing, he spun the empty tin cup from him and walked over where the elders were gathered around a buffalo-chip fire.

At his approach, the Quahada women moved behind their men. He understood that, their thrown looks. My God, did they think he was going to surrender them to the Texans for killing?

Rooney trailed across at the same time and through him, patiently, Baldwin addressed the upturned, inscrutable faces. Rooney's Comanche was unhurried, mindful of the ceremony on which a Comanche doted. His talk was resonant and flowing, interspersed with signs which his square hands somehow transformed into graceful, fluid air-pictures.

Soon, Baldwin stepped back in conclusion.

There was the rustling clank of chains as Hard Shirt stood up, his restricted movements pathetically awkward. He looked gaunt, older. He wore no eagle feather; his braided hair was unkempt. He stood bent, wrists burdened. His skinny shanks resembled sticks thrust between hoops instead of shackles. Hard Shirt's reply was a tangle of Comanche and swift-running sign. He was spurning his horse-barn English, which Baldwin knew was a sure indication of anger.

Baldwin needed no interpreter: the women and children stayed with the men, Hard Shirt said. They would not be separated. If necessary, the Comanche men would fight Stone Heart's pony soldiers to keep their families together.

"Try harder to make him understand," Baldwin said to Rooney. "There will be a big fight early in the morning. Some will be hurt — probably killed — if they stay. Tell him some of the white men are drinking crazy water."

Rooney spoke, faster now, and Hard Shirt, as if seeking affirmation, addressed the other Indian men. Each stood to speak. It was formal and time-killing and often wandering, but it was Comanche, Baldwin realized, and necessary.

"It's no use, Lieutenant," Rooney said after the last Indian sat down. "They don't trust Texans. They say they'd rather take their chances with us."

"Point out it isn't right for the children to die, too."

"We love our children — we will all die together — here on the prairie," Rooney relayed as Hard Shirt replied in defiant Comanche and made the Plains Indian sign for "done" — fists together in front of his body and moved right to right, left to left, the little he could.

Baldwin refused to give up. "Bring up Sand Creek in 'sixty-four, in Colorado, when Cheyenne women and children begged for mercy and white men butchered them during battle."

Rooney tried and received the identical refusal. Hard Shirt was adamant.

Baldwin didn't notice Topah until she was slipping forward, near him. She grasped his right hand in both hers, while the black glitter of her eyes pleaded for protection.

"*Tejanos* — no *bueno*," she said. "Quahada kill *Tejanos. Tejanos* kill Quahada."

"We won't let them," Baldwin said and repeated it before he realized she didn't understand him.

Rooney spoke. Topah dropped her hands and returned behind the Comanche men. There she sent her silent appeal across to Baldwin.

"Do they savvy about the escort?" Baldwin asked. "Is that clear?"

"They do. It don't make any difference, Lieutenant."

"What if Miss Pettijohn went along? Would they go, then?' A white woman would give them extra protection, in addition to the escort. It was my thought all along to send her with them. Ask 'em."

Hard Shirt's replying hands were scornful, framed in the pushing away sign.

"That settles it," Baldwin conceded, feeling a heavier concern.

"Did the lieutenant really think they'd go?"

"Guess not — but the choice had to be theirs. Not mine. But I could still make them go."

"Maybe," said Rooney, elevating an eye. "If so, I can see about ten troopers against two hundred drunks bent on another Sand Creek, an' what was left o' the platoon protectin' the bucks."

"Too thin either way," Baldwin agreed, "and I wouldn't let the families go without an escort. Miss Pettijohn presents a different problem. I feel this man Quincy, who's in command, would pledge her his personal protection."

Hard Shirt was hobbling forward, an expectancy, a suggestion in his fawning manner as he stopped and slid his sly glance from the handcuffs to Baldwin.

"Want me to knock those irons off?" Rooney asked, wishing to.

"Give him a free hand to stir up more commotion? No — he stays as is."

Baldwin left abruptly, in no mood for

another lengthy Comanche harangue, but soon fell to a slower, preoccupied step. The Quahadas' fears were real, made vivid by past experiences and their own harsh treatment of white captives. And even were they willing to separate, was it prudent to send them forth with less protection than they now had? Judging by the renewed shooting and yelling, he now questioned Quincy's control of Kelso's fire-eaters, Quincy's promise of safe conduct for anyone except a white woman.

Rachel was standing at the rear of her ambulance, in the attentive attitude of one who tries to ascertain from a distance what is happening and finds the results unsatisfactory.

"I was trying to get them to let the women and children go on tomorrow, under escort. Separate them from the bucks. They refused. Maybe you gathered that?"

"I couldn't tell from here."

"What they do doesn't change your situation one bit. I want you to pull out of the train. Go back to Fort Richardson. I will detail Estep to go with you. The Texans will let you through. I will arrange your safe conduct so there will be no doubt. When you get to the fort, you can hire a driver and continue your journey to the agency."

"Thee makes it sound very simple for me."

"It's best."

She stood absolutely still. "What thee asks is impossible," she said in troubled refusal.

"Because the Indians are staying? Don't be foolish. They're afraid to go, and they have some grounds for fear. You're different. Nobody's going to hurt a white woman."

"Thee's ordering me?"

"I prefer to state it differently. It's the only sensible way out."

"Sensible! Lieutenant, I could never do that! What would the Indians think of me — quitting them now, just when they need me?"

"They don't need you at all. What they need is four companies of cavalry to save their necks. From the first day we started, you offered them friendship. You tried to help. Everything you did they threw back at you — Topah — the otter woman."

"Did the children, too?" she asked pointedly.

"I'm thinking of the older Indians," he hedged. "You don't owe them a thing."

"I think I do."

"Not your life." In his intense desire to impress that upon her, he moved in a step. She faced him stiffly and again he sensed her refusal. He said, "I am going to tell you just how it is. We are in for trouble, maybe severe fighting in the morning. A good many of those white men out there are drunk. Killing Comanches is a sport to them. A circus. And no white woman, not even a Quaker missionary, had better get in their way."

"Thee's made up thy mind what to do?"

"I have until daybreak, when the truce ends. Then we wait for them to come at us for the bucks or we make a move before they do."

She turned and went in a straying walk to the front of the wagon and paused, faced away from him. "I can't go," she said with a desperation.

"You can't stay."

"It's after we reach the reservation," she said, her conviction complete. "They would remember me as the white woman — the Jesus woman — who left them when the *Tejanos* — my own people — were going to kill them. My work would be ruined." She shook her head decisively. "No . . . if I left I would go on to my home in Austin. There to stay. My purpose ended. Not north on a useless trip to the reservation."

"You seem positive we'll get through."

"I feel we will somehow," she said and faced him.

"That's a powerful faith. I wish I could be as certain."

"It's also a faith in thee. In Sergeant Rooney and the other men."

"Your presence complicates the train's defense."

"Thee could leave as well as I. Take thy men and leave the Comanches. Let them die."

"It's our duty to stay."

"That reason alone?" She pressed the question softly, yet behind it he could feel the power of her will. Almost, it seemed, as if she had a concern for him. Her face, in shadow, had an expression that eluded and fascinated him. Too, he remembered, it was a question she had asked of him once before. Her persistence was irritating. She spoke again. "There's no other?"

"You're confusing duty with sentiment again. They don't go together."

"And I have *my* duty, Mr. Baldwin. It's here — like thy own. Can't thee see?"

"It won't do. I am . . ."

Baldwin was listening — he heard a distant sound. It picked up to a violent rumble. It was nearing rapidly, the swelling drumbeats of horses running.

He said, "Get down —" and when she hesitated, he all but threw her under the ambulance, and a moment afterward there came a flurry of shots and the answering rattle of pickets' carbines.

His arm was around her, pinning her down. He heard the whooping riders pound past the east side of the corral and continue south, their horse racket fading. And shortly the terse voices of the pickets could be heard calling to each other.

He drew her up to her knees and realized now how rough and sudden he had been. In that moment her face was so close he could feel her breath warm and uneven on his face. Her fingers gripped his shoulder for support. He still held her. She felt wonderfully light and smooth under the thin summer dress. The odor of her skin and hair filled his nostrils. Sounds of the aroused camp shut out. He was watching the blur of her face, her mouth. He bent his head. She seemed to draw toward him.

At the last moment she turned her face aside.

Just then Rooney's voice clanged, "Kick

out those goddamn fires!" And, "Lieutenant —"

Whatever the moment might have held, it was gone.

"Rachel," Baldwin said, helping her up, "I was going to make you leave with Estep. Now we know that's not even safe. Therefore, we will make out here." She said nothing. She continued to face him without speaking. Rooney called again and Baldwin turned in that direction, a quiet fury beginning to burn the pit of his stomach because Quincy had broken the truce or was unable to restrain his men. "Over here," he yelled.

Rooney appeared on the double, mouthing outrage. "I'd like to take after 'em."

"Maybe that's what they want."

First, they made the rounds of the wagons. A mule was down inside the circle. Rooney shot it. An ancient Indian woman was dead. She looked no larger than a bundle of loose buckskin beside the kicked-out fire. Around her body the women were wailing and crying, while the big-eyed children watched solemnly from a distance.

A new anger was seating in Baldwin: these people could not fight back.

He turned grimly for the picket lines. Sullivan, on the northeast outpost, reported the riders had walked their horses within fifty yards. Breaking into a run, they had fired toward the wagons and kept going, afterward to circle and return to camp.

Baldwin felt they would try again, if merely to harass the train. He doubled pickets on the east and west flanks.

The thought took outline as they walked back. He said suddenly, "Have the farrier knock off Hard Shirt's irons," and feeling the sergeant's astonishment and aware of the implication within the order, he added, "Hell, I'm not turning him over to the Texans. It's just if he has to die, let him go out like a warrior."

"Arm him, too?"

Baldwin would have sworn that Rooney favored it. He said, "Of course not — and make this plain. I will shoot him myself if he tries to leave the train."

"Is that all, Lieutenant?" the sergeant asked, lingering.

"For now, yes."

Baldwin understood Rooney's hesitation. Some action, some plan was expected of him and soon. What did the lieutenant propose to do? This was intolerable; it was going to get worse.

Scarcely had the metallic tappings of the farrier's tools ceased on the far side of the circle when Hard Shirt and the few other Comanche elders materialized before Baldwin. Hard Shirt stood in close and made hand signs meaning Charge and Scalp and *Tejanos*, indicating he would lead the old men in the fight on the prairie tomorrow.

"No," Baldwin said, shaking his head.

The sheer intensity of the Comanche's signs gave them eloquence. *I will fight the Tejanos alone, if Stone Heart hands me a gun. Gives me pretty blue pony soldier suit.*

"No," Baldwin replied.

Sneering contempt warped the pockmarked countenance. *Stone Heart — he is big coward.*

"Go back to your wagons," Baldwin said and motioned.

If you won't fight, Hard Shirt said, sticking to the insulting gestures, *you must learn how to dodge bullets like a Comanche, and you must tell your pony soldiers not to eat breakfast so if they are shot in the belly they will not get sick.*

He fell into a crouching stance, weaving, dodging nimbly from side to side, almost flattening, then jerking up, twisting. He

251

took a side-stepping lunge and raised his arm fiercely over an imaginary enemy. Finished, he stepped back and seemed to await Baldwin's approval.

Baldwin nodded and signed him to stay with his people and protect them, for all the men to do the same.

Hard Shirt's hands flew. *Without guns?*

There had been a proper time for endless Comanche oratory earlier in the evening. Baldwin's patience ran out. "No guns," he said. "Go."

If Stone Heart will not fight, maybe so he will have enough courage to steal the Tejanos' horses?

These last signs were like flung sand as Hard Shirt, arrogantly, led the elders back to the wagons.

Once more the camp was still. All fires out.

Baldwin, left alone, reviewed his original orders. They were broad, as Mackenzie had intended. He could act within the wide dictates of his own judgment, which he had done so far in carrying out the colonel's instructions. He permitted himself the bitter luxury of one reflection: the situation was one in which his career teetered. The killing of a single drunken frontier citizen attacking the train could ruin him, depending somewhat on the status or prominence of the person shot and the loudness of the ensuing political howls. For instance, it would be more serious should Quincy stop lead. Not so much should Kelso. Baldwin thought along this line and discovered it didn't matter. Three years ago he had stopped thirsting for personal glory.

Rooney moved out of the night and paused, and by that Baldwin knew he was being asked again for instructions.

"Figure our bully boys will listen to reason come daybreak?" Rooney asked.

"Not a chance."

"Me feelin's are the same. And it goes against the grain, it does, not fightin' back." He stood there deliberately, waiting.

"Rooney," Baldwin said, "can you grease wagons by moonlight?"

"By moonlight? Huh, I could do it blindfolded in the bottom of a black cellar with one boot stuck in the mud and both me hands tied."

"I thought so. We sounded pretty noisy this afternoon."

"The lieutenant wants it done?"

"Yes."

"We'll get right on it."

"Fine."

Rooney paced off two slow steps and lingered. "Just uh what might the lieutenant be conjurin' up now?"

"Nothing brilliant, I regret. Only I know we're not going to squat here. Await their damned pleasure. Bring Corporals Higgins and Pierce over before you start the greasing."

Waiting, Baldwin chewed on an unlighted cigar and faced north where the citizens' camp lay, marked by a line of scattered fires. He could tell they were still whooping it up over there. As he watched and listened, his mind turned doggedly. He was not a superstitious man, but sometimes along the weary march he had felt that a strange order of events had conspired to thwart his progress. Every barrier had been succeeded by a progressively more formidable one, until he found himself hemmed in, surrounded, unable to run or maneuver.

As he thought of the camp blocking escape across Red River, it settled in his mind that he had overlooked the river's proximity. Only eight or ten miles, open all the way. He saw too that his thinking had been frozen in the opposite direction, to the south and the nearest source of help at Fort Richardson, which was out of reach.

Even should he ease a rider through, which wasn't likely, a relief column couldn't reach the train in time.

Several half-formed plans rose. He sorted them out detail by detail and discarded them one by one. He paced around the wagon and back and stood still. Quite suddenly, something Hard Shirt had said crossed his thoughts, and another way shaped. He forced it aside like the others; it returned, tenacious, determined, temptingly simple — and also the most dangerous, for he would be courting a general fight.

Not long afterward Rooney and Pierce and Higgins stood at ease before him.

"We can't outrun them," Baldwin said, "and we can't slip away. What I have in mind won't be found in Cooke's *Tactics*. About an hour before daybreak — because daybreak is when they will be expecting us to surrender the bucks — we will harness up, form the train in column of twos and proceed straight north." He held up, gathering his thoughts another moment.

"North?" said Higgins in wonder.

"That's right. I believe they would expect us to run away from them, instead of at them. The wagons of Miss Pettijohn and the Indians will be placed in the center. I

want to bust right through their camp —
on the run. I realize, of course, that getting
in close before we're discovered is the
tricky part. . . . Higgins, your worry will be
to see that no wagon lags behind. Rooney,
yours is to take the train on to the river
ford. Keep going. If a wagon breaks down,
distribute your people to other wagons.
But keep on. Start crossing as soon as you
can."

Hearing the plan aloud, Baldwin thought
it sounded foolishly bold and deficient in
judgment.

"Unless we keep this mob afoot," he
said, "we'll just end up in a running fight.
Mounted, they could cut us off from the
river and force a stand. Pierce, that's where
you and I come in. As the head of the train
breaks clear of their bivouac, you will be
on the left wing and myself on the right.
We will fan out with details and scatter
their horses. Instead, I should say drive
'em. Drive them hard to the river. Afterward, we swing in on the train in the vicinity of the ford, forming on Higgins' rear
guard."

Rooney said, "Now it makes sense," and
Baldwin had to smile at his candor.

"I should tell you," Baldwin said in the
same vein, "that I've had the benefit of a

mighty slick horse thief's advice tonight. It was Hard Shirt who suggested we take the horses. In fact, he dared me."

They talked on, gravely, going over the details. Rooney held out for dumping forage to lighten the heavier wagons and won. Presently the noncoms moved to depart.

"Wait," Baldwin said on impulse. He felt strangely embarrassed, unsure as how to express himself. "I want to say something. . . . I know how it's been. Plain hell most times. But we've stuck together. I am grateful for what you've done. You are honest-to-God, hard-tailed cavalrymen. That goes for every man in the platoon." He made a gesture. "And Conklin and Daily, back there . . . Rooney, I'd like you to pass that word, if you will. Some way."

The noncoms stood in silence, left awkward and stiff by his words. They stood so long that suddenly Baldwin wished they would go.

"Sure, Lieutenant," said Rooney.

Baldwin watched them moving off among the wagons, as phrases he couldn't summon moments ago flooded his mind. He had told them without thinking, but he had meant every word and much more that he couldn't say. He believed, and he hoped, they understood that a little.

Around eleven o'clock the horsemen swept past the train again, whooping, shooting. Alert picket fire forced them to ride farther out than previously. Except for the nuisance value and keeping the column awake, there was no loss the second time.

After leaving the outposts, Baldwin angled back to the corral. He scowled at the perfect, moon-pale night, its stars embossed like silver on the Spanish saddle of the sky. That glow had enabled his pickets to spot the horsemen; it would be equally revealing when the hooded wagons were in motion.

He hesitated upon nearing the Pettijohn wagon — and turned in on deliberate steps, thinking to remind her of certain precautions. She wasn't in sight. He felt a keen disappointment and was walking by when he saw her cross in front of the ambulance from the other side. Her hair glowed in the soft light. She showed no hesitation, causing him to wonder if she had been waiting for him to pass on his rounds.

"Estep tells me we're leaving," she began.

"In a few hours. Going to break out of here."

"I understand," she said and went on in a rush. "I thought — I mean I was thinking — if thee wishes I shall leave my supplies."

"Going to teach school, aren't you?"

"Yes — but —"

"So keep everything."

"I can have other supplies sent."

"Might take months. And you can make immediate use of those boxes and crates by putting yourself and some squaws and children behind them." He had referred to the school and its frontier necessities in a somewhat bantering tone. That was gone when he spoke next, in his direct, unvarnished way. "I won't tell you again to stay down. They'll start shooting the moment they discover us."

"That poor Indian woman this evening," she said. "How much easier it would be for thee if only the Indian men were along."

"As that is not the case, I can't see the logic of talking about it."

"I have multiplied thy burdens," she continued, her soft voice unchanged. "I have. I know. Haven't I?"

"This is hardly the time for self-reproach, Miss Pettijohn."

"It's the truth!" she flashed, contrite.

"All right, if you insist on the truth," he said, outspoken. "I didn't want a hymn-singing missionary — a woman, above all — on this train. I hate stale platitudes. I thought you would complain every step of the way. I expected you to rile up the Quahadas until I had to restrict you from any contact with them. Well, you've never complained — not once. You — you have been a great help with the Indians. That is the truth. I'm glad you came."

She regarded him for a long moment before overcoming her surprise. Then she said, "Thee's forgotten Topah and the otter woman."

"I've thought about that, too. No woman — certainly no medicine woman — wants to lose her influence. That was the main issue. You were helping and she got jealous. I don't believe Topah complained."

Baldwin wasn't aware how long they had been talking, how long they had stood on the same spot without moving; moreover, his excuse for returning was just half true. A powerful desire to see her had drawn him back, an incompleteness. Their conversation had grown more broken, more difficult. And somehow the night was different. It seemed to ebb and flow with a gossamer, web-like quality. There was a feel about it and a wonderful languor. It seemed impossible that just to the north a destruction was posed which could sweep everything about him away. The train was quiet again except for the incessant keening of the squaws, and now he forgot those sounds. He wondered what was happening to him. He felt acutely alive again. He saw Rachel's face as a pale flower.

He said, "You know, you've grown up since we left Fort Concho. There was a great deal of the zealot in you when we started. The hard-headedness of an army mule. Believe me! Such as your stand on Comanche morals." He stopped, primed for her protests. But she was silent. "You were a girl then," he said half-belligerently. "Now you're a woman and you don't even know it and I'm wondering why in heaven's name I'm telling you at a time like this."

What he said might have come from another person. He stopped on that, astonished at himself.

"It's not like thee to leave a thing unfinished, Mr. Baldwin," she said when he didn't go on.

He crossed the short distance between them. He found his hands on the rounded points of her shoulders and, incredibly, while he watched the liquid of her eyes, he saw her face turn not away from him as before but lift toward him. His arms became almost rough. The sudden feel of her slimness was a shock traveling over him and with it he sensed her wanting and giving and also the mystery of her.

Obviously, Rachel wasn't accustomed to kissing. Her lips, while full and warm, were unpracticed and hesitant, as if restrained by the curb of strict convention. That was his immediate sensation — it passed swiftly as he felt them settle and form with the pressure of an astonishing sweetness. He seemed blinded. His senses were swimming. He got the cleanness and fragrance of her hair as he turned his head aside while he held her. In his ear her breath came in quick little gasps.

"I don't know how it will be in the morning," he said.

"Thee will be there. I won't be afraid."

"You must do as I've told you."

"I will."

"There isn't much time to tell you these things."

"I love thee," she said simply and put her warm arms around his neck and drew his face down to hers.

Out of the night a voice invaded his consciousness. It was Rooney calling him.

Baldwin kissed her mouth, her cheeks, her eyes, her hair and her lips again. "Rachel," he said, "this happened long ago and I didn't know it." There was wonder and urgency in his voice, impelled by the fear that time might run out before he could tell her.

Rooney called again, insistently.

Baldwin dropped his arms, looked once at her face and walked toward the sound of Rooney's voice.

Chapter 12

The moon had taken another stride across the starry sky before Baldwin had time to think what had happened to Rachel and himself. Sleep was no longer possible; the hour was late. His mind was tossing, harassed by a remembered anguish. He felt the sudden lock of fear. What if something happened to her? That concern grasped him and did not diminish its hold as he watched the night advance in half-step. And there were the others as well.

Sometime around three o'clock he rose and gave the command to harness up, and heard the hum and stir of the camp begin all around him, muffled, small-scale sounds, stirring momentarily his recollections of weary columns moving into position before dawn through the Georgia pine barrens. He waited impatiently for order to arrive out of the congested milling; careful, hurrying voices, buckles snapping and the whip of cinches, the hoof trampings and snufflings — so loud he wondered if the preparations could go unnoticed.

He formed his few details, and was dismayed at the thin strength he had to distribute. He sensed more than saw the column's coming to a hushed readiness; cautiously, rubbing on greased axles, the first two wagons swung out to form the double file.

He saw the others trailing after, becoming links in a chain of hooded white. At that exact moment he had the vivid illusion of figures struggling across the dark canvas of land and sky. It seemed incongruous to feel the warm May wind playing against his face, to be smelling the mingled scents of sweet prairie.

On his right rode Mueller, bugle dangling. Behind them pressed the detail's handful.

Now all wagons were in jingling motion. A pinch of time worked by. Baldwin, tense to the low but audible rumbling of the train, watched the murk ahead. He searched for shapes, for movement. He saw none, he heard no sounds of alarm. He thought, "Are we going to surprise them completely?"

His answer came in moments, but it was behind him.

Hoo — kaaa — yaaaa!

He jerked around with a curse. The whoop seemed from Hard Shirt's wagon. Another yell tore loose. He was certain then as he caught sight of a gesturing figure. The yell was like a fuse, setting off more Comanche cries.

Instantly, Baldwin's mind switched to the column's head, for they were still out a distance from the camp. He bellowed at Mueller, whose trumpet was already raised.

"Sound the charge!"

At the scrambling rat-a-tat-tat, mules and horses lunged forward and the wagons, moving serenely, were yanked into violent swayings.

Baldwin spurred his detail up even with the lead wagons. A tremendous din was drumming his ears.

They kept running in that closed-up, precipitate order, faster, to the screeching accompaniment of the Quahada bucks and the high falsettos of the squaws and even the higher cries of the children. Ahead was only the uncertain light into which they rushed. Nothing more until Baldwin saw the speckling gun flashes, and quickly, almost underfoot, men leaping up from blankets and dodging or crouching or turning to fire at the white mass bursting upon them.

A figure, rifle swinging, barred his mount's path. Baldwin rode straight into him and felt a bump as the man cried out and rolled. He saw kicked bedrolls flying. There was the clumping bang of trampled coffee pots and skillets, the tinny clatter of trod tinware sent spinning, of men shouting in panic, and the fainter crash of shattered bottles. All the time Mueller's eager trumpet was venting its staccato notes.

Baldwin was straining for a glimpse of the picketed horses as the nose of the train broke clear. He saw them at once, as high-backed, scattered shapes — not bunched as much as he'd hoped. He raised a massive shout and wheeled the detail right.

Full voice, they all cut and went pouring across. It was a furious, sweeping movement, drumming terror and confusion. Before them the whistling, terrified picket animals were rearing and jerking and tearing free. Dimly, Baldwin made out a few men hanging desperately on the ends of ropes. Others crouched down, snapping shots at the troopers.

He sensed something was wrong just when the detail started down the camp's length, turning the horses toward the river. No longer did he hear the brassy excitement of Mueller's bugle; it was silent. He glanced quickly, in dread.

Mueller, until then riding steadily on his right, wasn't there.

There wasn't time to slow or wheel back. Yelling, the troopers tore on after the horses. A scattering was breaking back despite the drive's momentum. Most of them the detail succeeded in cutting in again, Baldwin saw, but some slipped through.

Pretty quick they were past the camp and running the big bunch north for the river, angling away from Rooney's line of march northwest to the ford, crowding it through a many-layered, mealy light over the dipping swells of prairie. Baldwin pushed hard. Once started, the horses drove without great trouble. When an animal did break, the spaced-out troopers cut it back.

There had to be a slowing down off the break-neck pace. When it came, Baldwin rode alongside Sullivan.

"What happened to Mueller? Anybody see?"

"Saw him drop back of a sudden. When

I looked again, he wasn't anywhere."

Baldwin accepted that with a drop of his head and rode on, seeing the flashes again as they raced along the camp's edge. Their ride and that of Pierce's detail had drawn attention away from the train as planned, provided diversions on the flanks. Baldwin had seen the wagons breaking through.

Young Mueller had helped make that possible. Mueller and his bugle. The trumpeter's cheerful, rather sensitive face returned to Baldwin; his manner of sounding a call, making it swell, mellow, unbroken, brassy or muted, always clear. Like sad music. And it was a music, meant only for distant, violent places; so it was this early morning. Mueller's people lived in Iowa; a girl was back there. Baldwin thought, "I will write them about him," and discovered a terrible shortage within himself. He knew very little about Mueller. Rooney was the only man in the platoon he really knew.

Haste took hold. Baldwin considered quitting the horses and circling around to Rooney. Yet, if he did now, he knew such impatience might wreck things. Not all the horses had been driven off. If quit this close to camp, these could be repossessed and the train possibly cut off before Rooney reached the ford.

He increased the pace, driving the troopers and himself. Behind them, south and off west, where Rooney was hurrying the wagons, there wasn't a crack of sound, not a gunshot. He strained to listen above the hoof rumble and asked if the silence meant an ominous lull.

A growing pink flushed the east when they bunched the horses down to the damp, sandy bottomland of the Red and into its scattered cottonwoods. Daylight was stripping away the night's murk. On the river's far side, the broken face of the bluff was revealed against the changing sky. The troopers looked haggard and grim in the gray light. Yelling, waving, jumping their mounts, they drove the horses into the brownish water, starting them for the other side. Those that managed to cut away or leave the swimmers, they let scatter down river. It would take hours to round them up.

Baldwin barely paused. He drew the detail in and turned up river, west. They rode doggedly, while the rising sun warmed their backs. They rode through an enfolding silence in which nothing stirred, so still and edgy they seemed to travel a hollowed-out country. He scanned it with troubled eyes.

Inside an hour he stopped on the crest of a small rise overlooking the ford. He took his quick look and his mouth parted. Apprehension thickened in his throat like a sharp pain. There was nothing down there.

"We moved pretty fast," Sullivan said.

"We also had a long way to go," Baldwin said. "They should be here unless they ran into trouble."

Breakdowns and citizens catching loose horses jammed his mind while he saddled south along the ruts of the old military road. What was keeping Rooney? He wasn't the kind who could be bluffed, and any fighting would have been audible.

About a mile onward Baldwin saw mules bobbing over a slope, and after them the whitetopped wagons in double file. He felt the rapid pump of relief as he rode to Rooney on the right flank.

"Two wagons broke down; had to shift around some," the sergeant informed Baldwin and spoke darkly. "Got bees in our tailfeathers."

"How many?"

"Thirty or forty, Higgins says. Looks like they plan to jump us at the ford; they're just follerin' along."

"Where's Pierce?"

"Just came in."

Baldwin hated to say it: "Rooney, we lost Mueller."

Rooney pinned Baldwin a straight-through look. The sturdy bow of his chest expanded and sank. Baldwin saw regret, then actual pain in the blue eyes. Rooney nodded. "He was a good lad — as good as we ever had." At once he said savagely, "Lieutenant, let Higgins ramrod the train across. I'd like to stay behind with ye."

"I understand," Baldwin said, shaking him off, "but we need you with the wagons."

"Is the river up?" Rooney asked slowly.

"Some. We can make it."

"River don't worry me much, Lieutenant. It's that domned long stretch o' sand a man fights gettin' to it."

"Keep going. We'll fall back with Higgins to cover the crossing."

More wagons passed. Baldwin saw Rachel riding in front with Estep. She waved and he rode across. An Indian woman and two blackeyed children peered out from under the canvas curtains. Rachel looked anxious, yet calm. She was smiling at him; that was another wonderful way she had. She could look into the unwelcome face of things and accept what had to be done. Her lips formed to speak. What she said was lost when Estep's whip cracked and the ambulance lurched.

Baldwin took the detail rearward to join the few of Higgins and Pierce. In the distance followed a clump of horsemen, beyond carbine range. They hovered at just that distance.

"They pull up when we do," Higgins explained. "Come on when we move."

Baldwin's glasses revealed an unexpected turn. Quincy wasn't leading the diehards. Kelso rode in front, a grim cast to his sharp features. His presence meant rashness; it meant a fight.

Of that Baldwin was convinced when he dismounted his men on the rise above the ford, sent horseholders to the rear and prepared for a stand.

On the sandy river bottom below, the scene resembled a swarm of toiling ants. Baldwin saw the Quahadas leave the wagons — women, the old men and children — and begin pushing and tugging and seizing the spokes of mired wagon wheels, laboring beside troopers and whipwielding drivers while the *wheeehawwwing* mules struggled in the sand. Progress was slow. They would heave and drag a wagon free only to have it sink again; the double column became a single line by necessity, leapfrogging forward by sections.

Even so, Rooney had the first wagon in crossing when Kelso's men, bunching suddenly, rode within carbine range.

Baldwin chewed his lip and decided to wait them out, yet hoping their purpose was to dash in, and away, hoping that such a demonstration of braggodocio, and having pursued to the river, might salvage reputations and satisfy Comanche hate.

Kelso, apparently, had firmer intentions. On the riders surged.

Baldwin caught Higgins' questioning glance for an order. He shook his head: wait.

Was Kelso bluffing? Baldwin couldn't tell yet.

They kept coming hard, yelling and raising a horse racket. They drove straight for the kneeling troopers — and, when only some forty yards away, wheeled loosely and went streaming past on a disorderly front, as taunting as Comanches. Out of the mass came an empty bottle spinning in the troopers' direction.

Baldwin thought, "Don't they know we'll fight?"

He watched them bunch and turn and start back, Kelso in the van. Baldwin hoped they would slant past again. When, instead, they rode straight as if massing for a charge, he gave an order.

"Fire one round over their heads."

Spencers banged, powder smoke bloomed and the riders slacked; when no one fell, they came on again. Kelso held a fast trot. He wasn't swerving.

At the same time Baldwin heard sputtering bugle notes. He listened in astonishment. Mueller flashed across his mind, and he felt the whip of a violent feeling.

Still, he waited.

Higgins darted him an urgent plea. There was a stretch of uneasy inaction as Kelso's men narrowed the distance; just the drumming and the galling discord of Mueller's trumpet. Was Kelso going to bluff to the last, then run over them? Was he going to turn? Baldwin saw that he wasn't. And he heard Kelso's men start shooting.

"All right — fire!" Baldwin yelled.

Thereafter, the clash was as savage as it was senseless. Powder smoke made patches of white fog, fell acrid on the tongue. Lead struck the earth in a dimpling rain. Baldwin saw a trooper sag gently forward. Higgins jerked from the smash of a bullet and sat back, his eyes sprung wide.

Baldwin wasn't aware when Kelso's

charge lost its momentum. He noticed no actual wavering, no turning tail. But pressing off his shots, he saw saddles emptied and men hanging on, hit, and loose horses running. By then the riders were sliding away, in bunches, and singly, breaking, frantic, quirting, spurring, terribly and astonishingly hurt.

"Hold your fire," Baldwin called. It quit on both sides, so near in unison it could have been by the same command.

A bitter perception swelled as Baldwin watched them scatter out of range: they had tried to bluff their way through to the wagons; if failing in that expecting hardly more than token resistance from so few. Hence, the incident he had struggled to avoid, and which he now sensed old-soldier Quincy hadn't wished, had happened after all.

Tiredly, he ordered the wounded packed down to the sandy ford to be loaded on the wagons.

Chapter 13

Climbing the final yards of the shaly bench above the tawny river, Baldwin was met by an impression of vast space. Before him opened an emerald world, bright, limitless, rolling; it pitched gently northward toward Fort Sill, still more than a day's journey. Land and sky seemed to merge in the burnished distance where a long-running ridge rose to the pleased eye. Upon the prairie, gleaming whitely, stretched the parallel bands of the military road, beckoning, drawing the gaze. Everything suggested an immense peace. He could see the end by tomorrow, at last.

As he paused on top to wait for the straggling troopers, he experienced a sudden and irrepressible humility. Yet with it came a calm, powerful feeling of elated wonder. Even though the red waters hadn't parted for the fleeing wagons and covered up the enemy's horsemen, another miracle had happened. Yes. He knew. He saw it as an absolute blade of truth striking straight through his mind. Something unbelievable had occurred — Indians and troopers forgetting their pounded-in differences to stand together. He saw it while admitting the instrument of a common threat. But the beginning was far back down the trail. And who could say where? When Rachel tried to help Topah? When she and Rooney played with the children of Israel on the spongy banks of the Brazos?

The troopers closed up and he led them ahead, warmed at the turn of his discovery.

He rode unhurriedly to the wagons, assembled in single file, an alignment indicating that Rooney figured the worst was over. Rooney waited on a drooping horse. He sat slumped, not moving. Weariness smudged his eyes, his sunburned cheeks. No man had toiled harder than he in the sand. Somehow he looked smaller, older. Baldwin, with a pang, realized Rooney's usual actions belied his age by years. Only rarely, as now, on the edge of exhaustion, did the cruel past catch up.

But something more warned Baldwin, a hesitancy in the sergeant's manner. His tone was burdened and pushed out when he spoke, as if there was yet another river to be crossed or another battle to be fought.

"Hard Shirt's in a bad way, Lieutenant. I just found out. All shot up. Got it comin' through the camp. Wouldn't stay down. Might know. Th' domned old cuss had to stand up, holler at the *Tejanos*. Let 'em know he wasn't afraid."

They rode to the Indian's wagon and dismounted. The letdown tailgate enabled Baldwin to see him lying on a bed of blankets, his head slightly raised. Wives and children hovered close, their dark eyes revealing the concern their silence hid. Topah rose to leave, but sat down again when Baldwin made the stay sign.

Hard Shirt's appearance was startling. His wrinkled face, painted for war, looked hideous with streaks of black, the symbol of death. Vermilion underlaid the black lines; an eerie white daubed his eyelids. Except for the stained bandages across his chest, which Baldwin guessed Rooney had supplied, Hard Shirt was a brilliant, blue-dotted yellow from neck to waist. His breathing was a short, labored rasp. The harsh slash of his mouth was set against pain. He did not complain by word or look. His gaze on the white men was unwavering.

"Tell him we will camp here a while so he can rest," Baldwin said, catching Rooney's eye.

Rooney and Hard Shirt talked briefly, the Indian preferring Comanche, it seemed, because of the less effort.

After which Rooney said, "He says this is a bad place. *Tejanos* might cross the river. So go on. Anyway, he is very tired. He longs to see his old friends at the agency before he dies. His bed in the wagon is soft. He has wives to wait on him. He says go on. Hurry fast."

Baldwin nodded his agreement. He turned. But Hard Shirt, who had spoken without raising a hand, made a small gesture. Baldwin paused and saw, flaring weakly, the old arrogance. Hard Shirt motioned Baldwin closer.

"Stone Heart," the Comanche breathed as Baldwin leaned in, "no *bueno* pony-stealer, huh? *Tejanos* catch up. Big fight." Amusement flecked the black eyes. There was one difference, Baldwin thought: the usual scorn wasn't evident. Well, not all of it.

"You —" Baldwin's hands conceded, taking in the four great directions — "you — Hard Shirt — are greatest Comanche pony-stealer."

Pleasure overspread the painted features.

280

Hard Shirt jogged his head up and down, acknowledging, savoring the praise.

Again, Baldwin turned to go and again, by gesture, he was summoned back.

Hard Shirt's gaze centered, fixed wistfully on Baldwin's blouse. He reached out a veined hand. "Nice," he said, stroking the blue sleeve. "Heap nice." Slowly, reluctantly, the plucking hand slipped down, Hard Shirt sank back, spent, and Baldwin straightened. He and Rooney walked quietly to their horses.

As the day fell away into late afternoon, the air turned heavy and a grayish tinge replaced the spring sky's bright hue. Southwest, Baldwin saw the dark hedges of clouds. And the wind changed, its breath sultry. The Indians, knowing the familiar signs, watched with apprehension; and as Hard Shirt grew weaker, they seemed to detect an ominous connection in the black cloud banks marching toward them.

Baldwin didn't hesitate when he saw the swaying greenery of West Cache Creek's elms and cottonwoods. His teams were played out, his people as well. He stood in his stirrups and pointed and made the circling motion for camp, sending the wagons into bivouac along the sheltering creek behind a low hill.

Too warm, too moist on the skin, the sluggish wind was rising when Baldwin, just dismounted, noticed an Indian woman running. It was Topah, her cropped hair flying. Her dark eyes were wild as she ran up and seized his arm and gestured back, pleading in Comanche.

Her meaning was plain. He nodded that he would go. She was running back before he could tie his horse.

It seemed right to find Rachel at the Hard Shirt wagon. Baldwin stepped up beside her and looked in.

Hard Shirt lay as he had when Baldwin saw him after crossing the river. Only his bandages were stained all through. Only he was much weaker, Baldwin noted, and made no effort to raise his head, propped under a rolled blanket. Unlooked for was the unshakable calm that suffused the painted, hideous face; it marked even the sunken eyes, which now slid from Baldwin, after lingering on the uniform, and singled out Rachel.

"I believe he wants to tell you something," Baldwin said.

As she moved to the end of the wagon and her hands pressed against the tailgate, Baldwin's impression of savagery and painted symbols faded. Hard Shirt's fierce face seemed transformed, the cruel eyes soft and glowing.

"My friend," the Indian addressed Rachel, his voice studied and difficult. It occurred to Baldwin that Hard Shirt was speaking white man for her benefit alone, because she knew no Comanche.

"My friend — I can — see your heart."

Rachel was startled. She pressed a hand to her throat.

Hard Shirt raised himself a little. "Your heart heap *bueno*. You love Quahada. Love ever'body. *Tejanos* come — you stay. No run. Brave. Your medicine good." A fit of coughing overwhelmed him. He was spent, only the glowing coals of his eyes showing life.

Pity and wonder mixed in Baldwin.

Rachel was rigid, intent, absorbed, hurting.

"No hurt Jesus woman." Hard Shirt, weaker, had to pause. "Quahada — all Quahada — all Comanche — love Jesus woman."

Rachel was weeping softly as he finished, as he lay back with shuttered eyes. Topah, dry-eyed, had a contorted fear on her face, an acceptance, resignation.

Almost before he knew it, Baldwin was removing his blouse. He shed it deliberately and handed it to Topah, who stared back, not comprehending, not taking, until he offered again. Topah's face softened in understanding and she turned with the blue coat, calling.

Baldwin stepped back and walked away.

It wasn't long before he heard the high wailing sounds commence and spread, striking among all the Quahada wagons.

That evening the pursuing dark clouds caught up and throughout the night assailed the train with rain and thunder and lightning and gusty winds shrieking off the short-grassed Comanche prairie. At daybreak the sky was clear, spun clean by its own violence, shining with promise.

Taking the wagons onward again, Baldwin thought of Hard Shirt's burial as part of the preliminary turmoil. Comanches weren't afraid to die: after all, they lived in a world of daily uncertainty and danger. To them the most important thing in life for a man was to be brave, to die in battle or to receive a mortal wound while fighting, which was a joy. But brave as they were the dead made them nervous, and Hard Shirt, that mighty fighter and noted horse thief, was already conveniently painted. Therefore, hurriedly, before the storm struck, they had placed him, sitting, on a horse, an Indian buck behind, and buried him among the rocks of a draw where he could face the rising sun. Buried him proudly in the blue blouse, which was another mark of a warrior.

Strangest, Baldwin thought, overspreading everything that had happened, was Rachel's indisputable triumph of love.

Meanwhile, he permitted no letup this last day. He drove the train hard.

At noon he dispatched Private Sullivan to inform the agency and fort officials of the train's afternoon arrival and the death of Hard Shirt. In doing so Baldwin ran against certain sobering facts:

Tejanos had killed Hard Shirt and the Indian woman; by custom, by honor, relatives and friends must conduct revenge raids below Red River against the settlements until they felt a sufficient number of scalps — any Texan's would do — had been taken to satisfy the losses. He could foresee only vindictive wrath from the agency Indians. Furthermore, in failing to deliver his principal prisoner alive, his mission was a failure.

As the great eye of the sun sagged lower and the irregular line of the Wichita Mountains was traced low across the northwestern sky, he felt an actual dread of the escort's reception at the agency. He kept seeing sullen bucks and wailing, weeping relatives, who would blame the pony soldiers. Everybody Indian mad! Also he was beginning to find a complete exhaustion of mind and body within himself.

Consequently, he jerked with tautness when an Indian rider appeared ahead of the train, watched some moments, spotted pony dancing, and raced swiftly back. But not before Baldwin noticed the Indian's rifle.

Nothing happened for several minutes, causing Baldwin to read further suspicions in the rider's behavior. If he was friendly, why had he run? Why was he armed? In the past, small detachments of cavalry had been attacked while in vicinity of the fort, and Quaker employees of the agency terrorized.

Still, he was surprised by the suddenness and number of the riders when they popped into view over a long slope. Indians. He missed Mueller now; so by the time his flankers were hand-signaled in and posted around the train and the rear guard formed in also, the Indians were within revolver range: too close to form a corral.

They seemed to spring out of the May-time air with squalling cries, quirting, heel-clapping Indians on flashing bays and paints and roans, Indians with red-and-white headdresses flowing in the warm wind, Indians carrying rifles and bows and arrows.

Baldwin and Rooney fell back on the lead vehicle, weapons at the ready.

But instead of driving straight down upon the train, the Indians fanned aside and went racing along its west flank, firing guns, whooping a din which the command's mules, most of them conditioned by that frightening night below Fort Chadbourne, reacted to by rearing and trying to spook.

Baldwin, watching, suddenly holstered his revolver. These Indians were peculiar ones indeed; they were firing over their heads.

"Hell — it's a reception, Lieutenant!" Rooney shouted in relief.

So it was, the likes of which Baldwin had never witnessed before and did not understand. His astonishment grew.

Traveling as fast as their wild-eyed ponies could jump, the Indians swept to the train's rear and around, yipping like playful coyotes as they poured up the east side.

They began riding all over the ponies, some hanging on the off side, some turning somersaults or riding faced to the rear or standing erect. One young buck was hanging under his horse's belly. All the time they were yelling and the Quahadas in the wagons answering back.

Never easing up, the band drummed past Baldwin and on north until a dip in the prairie swallowed them.

The agency was close and presently Baldwin sighted buildings scattered like brown blocks on the green floor of the prairie. And nearer, when the trail leveled off, he saw many things at once. A panorama of tipis and tents on the wide flat around the agency. Smoke raveling up from an astonishing number of cooking fires. Herds of grazing ponies. And Indians — masses of them, afoot and mounted, waiting. Almost lost in the crowd was a knot of Quaker families. Near them stood a detachment of infantry at ease.

Baldwin led the train on, and when the crowd moved to meet the wagons, he felt his dread rise again. Didn't they know Hard Shirt was dead? Had Sullivan failed to tell the agent? If so, had he, in fear, failed to inform the Indians?

Seeing there wasn't room for the wagons to advance without injuring someone, Baldwin halted.

Instantly, the Indians ran forward, and spilling down from the wagons, crying, calling, came the Quahada captives. They met in a crush of emotion. Baldwin turned away, affected by the cries and sights, and saw troopers also facing away.

It all left him uneasy and he looked around for the agent, thinking some kind of official transfer of the captives should be made. He thought that when, in fact, he knew his real wish was to get away from this place; for he was worn down, the mission was finished, and he wanted to avoid an angry demonstration.

He was still searching for the Quaker agent among the milling Indians when, like an enveloping wave, they overflowed around his horse and reached for his hand. An ancient Comanche, his teeth worn to the gums and his puckered countenance as wizened as a dried prune's, signed for Baldwin to dismount.

Baldwin hesitated — and obeyed slowly, on an odd sense of propriety, and was amazed to find the Indian, an enormous smile splitting his eroded face, shaking his hand violently, warmly. Baldwin felt himself clutched and hugged. Woodsmoke and grease smells came to his nostrils. Before he knew what to expect next, the other Indians were pumping his hand and embracing him. His hat fell askew; he pushed it back in order to see. He was startled to recognize Quahada faces from the train smiling at him, Quahadas hugging him. He knew vaguely that actions just as strange were going on by the wagons. Grinning Comanches shaking hands with the troopers; more Indians grouped about Rachel's ambulance.

Confused, bewildered, he turned in helplessness and saw he could not escape. Comanches merely grinned at his dilemma. His hand was being pumped again and all the Indians seemed to be jabbering simultaneously, when the old Indian man, who appeared to possess the air of official spokesman, uttered a piercing call. Gradually the uproar subsided. Indians cleared away from Baldwin. He stood free, alone except for the old one.

"Stone Heart," the Comanche said, pointing to Baldwin, "you — pony soldiers — make our hearts good. You guarded our families — you fed them. You fought *Tejanos* for them. Stone Heart — you are brave," and he cut the fluid sign for Brave and Strong, closed left hand held across his body and his right fist striking down past his left. "Your old name is used up — your new name is Stands Brave."

Baldwin felt heat on his face. He could not believe. He could only stare blankly when a boy led out a blood-red bay horse to the old man, who, with slow dignity, extended the reins for Baldwin to take.

He lagged, thinking to refuse. He had the swift thought: "Don't they know Hard Shirt is dead? Why haven't they been told?" And had his answer almost as he asked. These families were being united again: husbands with wives, parents with children, sisters with brothers.

He took the reins and immediately he was swarmed again, as if on signal. Not one by one, but by a crush of Comanches. Men and women, they pressed their gifts upon him. Buffalo robes, buckskin shirts, quirts, blankets, beaded moccasins, vests, belts, gloves. Precious silver ornaments. A pathetic strip of trader's red cloth. An elderly woman laid a slab of government issue bacon at his feet.

His body was numb. He had no voice. He was dumfounded. He felt something wet skip down his cheeks. He was staring at the blurred lake of gleaming faces, unable to speak or make even the proper thanking signs because he held the bay's rope in one hand and his mount's in the other.

As suddenly as they had surrounded him they were streaming off toward the camps and the cooking fires, gone. With them the Quahada captives. He could see the bronzed children running like spring colts across the prairie, and then they also were gone. It came to him that he would miss them. He was conscious of stillness, of the lined-up wagons; already they looked forlornly empty.

He took a step to bring the horses about and stumbled on the piled gifts.

Looking up, he saw Rachel standing with the Quaker families. She was watching him. She was waiting, and he found again what he had glimpsed briefly in the choking dust of the deadly pass that day, yet different now because it was for him, the expression in the face that he could never think of again as plain.

About the Author

Fred Grove was born in Hominy, Oklahoma, and was graduated from the University of Oklahoma with a Bachelor's degree in Journalism. While working on newspapers in Oklahoma and Texas in the early 1950s, Grove began publishing short stories in some of the leading Western pulp magazines. His first four Western novels were published by Ballantine Books and include some of his finest work, especially *Comanche Captives* (1961) which earned him the first of five Golden Spur Awards from the Western Award from the University of Oklahoma and the Levi Strauss Golden Saddleman Award. *The Buffalo Runners* (1968) won the Western Heritage Award from the National Cowboy Hall of Fame.

Grove's Western fiction is characterized by a broad spectrum of different settings and time periods. *The Great Horse Race*

(1977) and *Match Race* (1982), both of which won Golden Spur Awards, are concerned with modern quarter horse racing. *Phantom Warrior* (1981) and *A Far Trumpet* (1985) are set during the time of the Apache wars. Two of Grove's most memorable novels, *Warrior Road* (1974) and *Drums Without Warriors* (1976), focus on the brutal Osage murders during the Roaring Twenties, a national scandal that involved the Federal Bureau of Investigation. *No Bugles, No Glory* (1959) and *Bitter Trumpet* (1989) are notable for their graphic settings during the Civil War. Grove himself once observed that "thanks to my father, who was a trail driver and rancher, and to my mother, who was of Osage and Sioux Indian blood, I feel fortunate that I can write about the American Indian and white man from a middle viewpoint, each in his own fair perspective . . ." Grove now resides in Tucson, Arizona, with his wife, Lucile, and has just completed *Man on a Red Horse* to be published as a **Five Star Western**.

We hope you have enjoyed this Large Print book. Other Thorndike, Wheeler or Chivers Press Large Print books are available at your library or directly from the publishers.

For more information about current and upcoming titles, please call or write, without obligation, to:

Publisher
Thorndike Press
295 Kennedy Memorial Drive
Waterville, ME   04901
Tel. (800) 223-1244

Or visit our Web site at:
www.gale.com/thorndike
www.gale.com/wheeler

OR

Chivers Large Print
published by BBC Audiobooks Ltd
St James House, The Square
Lower Bristol Road
Bath BA2 3BH
England
Tel. +44(0) 800 136919
email: bbcaudiobooks@bbc.co.uk
www.bbcaudiobooks.co.uk

All our Large Print titles are designed for easy reading, and all our books are made to last.